Save My Place

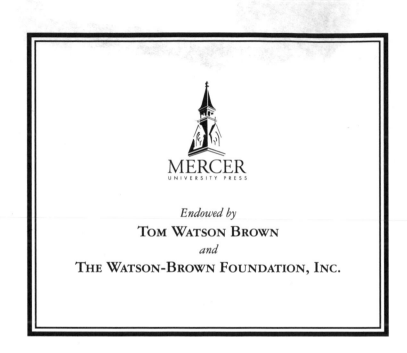

Endowed by
TOM WATSON BROWN
and
THE WATSON-BROWN FOUNDATION, INC.

Save My Place

A NOVEL

OLIVIA deBELLE BYRD

MERCER UNIVERSITY PRESS | MACON, GEORGIA

35 Years of Publishing Excellence

MUP/ 493

Published by Mercer University Press, Macon, Georgia 31207
© 2014 by Mercer University Press
1400 Coleman Avenue
Macon, Georgia 31207

9 8 7 6 5 4 3 2 1

Library of Congress Cataloging-in-Publication Data
Byrd, Olivia deBelle.
  Save my place : a love story / Olivia deBelle Byrd.
    pages cm
  ISBN 978-0-88146-501-3 (pbk. : acid-free paper)
  ISBN 0-88146-501-1 (pbk. : acid-free paper)
  ISBN 978-0-88146-503-7 (ebook)
  ISBN 0-88146-503-8 (ebook)
  1. Love stories. I. Title.
  PS3602.Y74S28 2014
  813'.6--dc23
                                                        2014015768

To Barbara,

my White Rose sister,

who has shown me how to live life with grace and courage.

With her popular book of essays, *Miss Hildreth Wore Brown: Anecdotes of a Southern Belle*, Olivia deBelle Byrd pulled at the funny bone of a multitude of readers. Now with her wonderful debut novella, *Save My Place*, she successfully pulls at the heartstrings. In a moving and grounded narrative voice, Byrd paints a portrait of new love, family secrets, unspeakable loss, treasured childhood memories, and redemption—all set against the backdrop of a changing world during the Vietnam War. *Save My Place* is as bright and uplifting as the Florida sun where the novel's protagonist, Elisabeth, retreats to mend the broken pieces of her life. It is not to be missed.

—Michael Morris, *Man in the Blue Moon*

Olivia deBelle Byrd is one of my favorite Southern writers—elegant, witty, and wise. In *Save My Place*, she employs all of those gifts to craft an epic love story that's sure to fire the imaginations and passions of her readers. This is a tremendously moving tale of romance, faith, and patriotism—and a great reminder of all that's true and lasting in life.

—Robert Leleux, author of
Memoirs of a Beautiful Boy and *The Living End*

The first thing I liked about *Save My Place* is the author's name: Olivia deBelle Byrd. If you can't make it as a writer in the South with a name like that, well, you're not really trying, are you? *Save My Place* is a charming read for almost anyone—young adult to senility. I'd be comfortable placing it in my Episcopal church library! It's a sweet love story about ordinary Southerners, Elisabeth and Kincaid—I promise you they are quite authentic characters—facing war and personal tragedy with fortitude and grace. And if you have a fondness for love letters like I do, this novel offers some gems—the best pages of the book, I think. Kincaid may have the most romantic theory about anniversary flowers I've ever heard in my life. I'm glad I spent some time with these pages.

—Melinda Rainey Thompson, author of
SWAG: Southern Women Aging Gracefully

Olivia deBelle Byrd is every bit as clever and utterly delightful as her writing suggests. *Save My Place* is a stirring story about hard times and lasting love and the God who never leaves us.

—Karen Spears Zacharias, author of *Mother of Rain*

Save My Place is a rare find, the kind of inspirational, old-fashioned novel you can't wait to recommend to your friends. Gracefully, tenderly, Olivia Byrd has penned an uplifting story of love, loss, and the courage to carry on despite the inevitable heartbreaks life brings our way.

—Cassandra King, *Same Sweet Girls Guide to Life*

In this world we move through shadows
Never sure of what we see
While the truth abides between us
Come and share the truth with me

Take my hand and lift me higher
Be my love and my desire
Hold me safe in honor bound
Take my heart to higher ground

Barbra Streisand
Higher Ground lyrics

Anon, to sudden silence won,
In fancy they pursue
The dream-child moving through a land
Of wonders wild and new,
In friendly chat with bird or beast—
And half believe it true.

Lewis Carroll
Alice's Adventures in Wonderland

Save My Place

Prologue

I had a dream last night. Like a kaleidoscope, a spinning array of brightly colored images burst forth one after another. It was springtime and my seven-year-old students were tumbling on the school playground while Jenny, wearing one of her flowered hats, watched. All at once, Karen arose from the entangled bodies of the children with young Colin in tow. When Colin saw me, he shouted with glee and came running, giggling, into my outstretched arms.

Out of the images, Curt appeared as angry as I had ever seen him. An unease sprung in the pit of my stomach seeing the out-of-place rage on his face in place of his usual jovial expression. Then Grandmother Reid was holding me in her strong arms as I lay sobbing in her lap. She was gently stroking my tangled hair saying in her calming voice, "It will be all right, Elisabeth Belle. Everything will be all right."

Suddenly, bombs began exploding, splintering trees and ripping apart the foliage all around me. I awoke trembling and sweating and from the wetness on my pillow I knew the tears were real. Fully awake now, fear gripped my heart as the thought came to me *what if Grandmother Reid is wrong.*

1

My stubborn Southern mind was made up. At the ripe old age of twenty-two, I was to become an old maid. Given that fact, I determined it was judicious of me to further my education, so I had taken the graduate exam and applied to the University of Georgia for a master's degree in education. Since the school was incidental to my momentous decision to enter the world of spinsterhood, the University of Georgia was selected based on the sole criterion of a college sorority sister who needed a roommate. This pivotal U-turn in my life was the indirect result of my college boyfriend of three years—the man I was to marry, settle down with in a cottage by the sea, and live with happily ever after—unceremoniously breaking up with me exactly twenty-four hours after my college graduation.

I attended college at Briarmore, a small liberal arts school in Birmingham, Alabama. Three weeks before I was to leave for college, my dentist, Dr. Fields discovered my wisdom teeth needed to be extracted. Since there was no oral surgeon in our small town, my father called a college friend of his who was a dentist in Birmingham for a recommendation. In the course of the conversation, Dr. Taylor mentioned his son Cameron would be a junior at Briarmore, and I should look him up. "No doubt about it, if parents are involved, this Cameron Taylor will be a nerd," I said to my parents with my usual sarcasm though I had to secretly admit his name sounded promising. I was an incurable romantic, and Cameron had a nice ring to it.

By sheer good fortune, I already had a friend at Briarmore. Isabella Sinclair, who was a sophomore, had begun writing me during the summer to welcome me to Briarmore, and we had discovered a mutual affinity for letter writing. We wrote copious epistles all summer, and by fall, Isabella was my new best friend. I pledged Kappa Delta, her sorority, and entered into all the initiation rites required of a pledge.

I was one of those children who loved the art of learning— the classroom was my playground. From the minute I sashayed into Mrs. Aultman's kindergarten, I reveled in everything about it. On the first day of kindergarten at recess, Sammy Pipkin told me to pump my legs on the swing so I could go higher, and sure enough, I felt like I was flying. The brightly colored alphabet cards that adorned the room beckoned to me, and I missed recess the day we colored a queen for Q so I could draw extra rubies and emeralds on her tiara. My queen was brightly hued and embellished but colored within the lines. It was already obvious I was creative and independent but not rebellious. Mrs. Aultman pronounced it the fanciest queen ever colored in her kindergarten, and I was quite pleased with my five-year-old self.

The first day of kindergarten when Mrs. Aultman called out my name I promptly spoke up. "My whole name is Elisabeth Belle Sterling, and it is spelled Elisabeth with an *s*."

"Well, aren't you the precocious one, Elisabeth Belle Sterling," Mrs. Aultman said.

As soon as I got home, I asked my mother what *precocious* meant. "It means you are clever and utterly delightful," my mother replied. That was a relief, because from the manner in which Mrs. Aultman had said it, I was not too sure. That started the word game with my father. All through my school years, I would present a new word to my father and then use it in a sentence as many times as I could that day. He told me to get my words from books and newspapers because they did not use really big words on television. I found *divan* in a Nancy Drew mystery and would prissily tell my parents, "If you need me, I will be sitting on the *divan* in the den reading a book." My favorite word became *ensconced* from *Wuthering Heights* until my parents begged me to quit using it. When my father and I played the word game, my pesky younger brother Stewart would gag and complain, "I'm completely surrounded by geeks."

"No, you're not, Stewart. You're surrounded by savants. You, on the other hand, are a Neanderthal." Since Stewart had yet to make it to the end of a book, he had no idea I had just insulted him.

College was another step in my education that I relished, so it was no surprise I fell immediately and unequivocally in love with Briarmore. I adored everything about it—the imposing red brick buildings, the distinguished, silver-haired professors, the lush, grassy quad, the din of the cafeteria. As soon as I got to Briarmore, I asked Isabella about Cameron Taylor. "You know Cameron Taylor?" she said with disbelief.

"Not really—our parents know each other."

"Elisabeth, Cameron Taylor is the best-looking hunk on campus. I am talking movie star gorgeous. Any girl at Briarmore would give her right arm to date him."

"You have to be kidding!"

"There's only one problem," Isabella said. I knew there would be a chink in his shining armor. "He tends to date girls on the wild side!" My miniscule hope immediately plummeted as I did not in any form or fashion walk on the wild side. To date, the most rebellious thing I had ever done was, at twelve years old and entering junior high, stuff my bra with toilet paper until I grew a decent set of breasts.

The first time I saw Cameron Taylor I could not believe it. Isabella, even with her penchant for drama, had not exaggerated. He was, quite simply, gorgeous. Cameron was over six feet tall with silky-blonde hair and smoky-blue eyes. He was on the swim team, so he had that exquisite chiseled body that swimmers seem to possess. As Isabella pointed out, "Every part of his physique seems sculpted to perfection." Isabella was an art major, so she used words like *sculpted*.

Since there were no sorority houses at Briarmore, the Kappa Deltas congregated at a designated table in the school cafeteria. It just so happened that the Sigma Alpha Epsilon table was close by, and Cameron was an SAE. I had never gotten up enough nerve to introduce myself, but a few times in the cafeteria I had looked up to see Cameron looking at me. He possessed great aplomb and would just smile until I self-consciously looked away.

The dress style of Southern coeds in 1965 was Villager skirts and V-necked sweaters accessorized with John Romain handbags while Weejun loafers adorned the feet. Uniformity was the rule of the day. Somewhere in the four years of college, we segued into a skirt/short combo called culottes worn with knee-socks, but we clung steadfastly to our Weejuns. Gant shirts, khakis, and *cords*, which was code for corduroy slacks, were *de rigueur* for male students. I could not help but notice, as the weather turned cooler, Cameron began wearing turtlenecks and cowboy boots. In a small Southern college like Briarmore this amounted to outright rebellion as it was a brave student who veered from our dress mantle of uniformity, but all this daring act did was add to the attraction and mystique of Cameron Taylor.

A senior rugby player named Norman Schneider had befriended our group of freshmen girls and had become our liaison into the world of upperclassmen. Norman's nose had been broken so many times playing rugby it gave him a rugged, gruff look, but he was as soft and kind as a koala bear. At

Christmas every year at the fraternity house, the SAE's had a lavish party for underprivileged children. Norman approached me in December. "Cameron Taylor wants me to find out if you would be interested in going to the SAE children's Christmas party with him."

My heart skipped entirely too many beats. "Are you kidding, Norman?"

"No, I am perfectly serious. Are you interested?"

Do I look like a complete moron? The best looking boy I had ever laid eyes on wanted me to go on a date. Of course, I was interested. But I nonchalantly said, "Sure, that sounds okay."

Cameron called me to confirm our date and picked me up at the dorm promptly at six. At the party, our child was a freckled-face, red-headed eight-year-old named Jack. I have always loved children, which is one of the main reasons I had become an education major, so Jack and I hit it off famously as he zoomed his new remote-control car across the floor and tossed a football with Cameron. Cameron later said that is when he fell in love with me—watching me play with Jack. After the moppets left, we had a few hours until curfew. We were sitting with Adam and Sarah, Cameron's best friend and his girlfriend, trying to decide what to do. I had just learned about a custom at Briarmore called creekbanking: a couple would take a blanket and go to a secluded place. It was assumed by most as an opportunity to make out, so when Adam and Cameron started talking about going creekbanking, Isabella's words about Cameron dating girls on the wild side began pressing on my mind. I was wondering if there was any way Cameron could possibly have gotten the wrong impression about me. I could not imagine how.

We did go creekbanking to a spot on the football field. My worries were unfounded as Cameron never even tried to hold my hand. We talked easily for two hours. We discussed our families, which seemed very similar, and Cameron told me about his goals and dreams for life. This was amazing to me, because up until this time, I did not realize boys actually had goals, and I thought their dreams mainly consisted of getting a girl to have sex with them. The only odd thing that happened was Cameron told me he never planned on getting married. Since I had never met a soul in the world whose future plans did not include marriage, I did not actually believe him. I was staying with Isabella that night, and as Cameron and I approached the sophomore dorm, he took the blanket and threw it behind some bushes. Surprised, I asked, "Why did you do that?"

"I wouldn't want anyone to think we were doing anything other than talking," he replied, and that is when I fell in love with Cameron Taylor. I loved his looks and he loved my sarcasm. I told Isabella she needed to learn CPR and accompany me to Cameron's swim meets because my heart stopped beating when I saw Cameron shirtless.

"And who's going to revive me?" she asked.

Despite his good looks, there was nothing arrogant or shallow about Cameron. He had more depth than any boy I had ever met. He was disarmingly charming but possessed a sensitivity that was irresistible. It turned out he was also keenly intelligent with a wonderful dry humor to match. He loved the fact I could do battle with his wit and match him barb for barb.

Cameron and I both loved the art of conversation. We spent hours discussing a myriad of topics—philosophy, religion, psychology, books, and his love, the Beatles. Movies were a fetish for us, and Cameron could dissect a scene or line of dialogue like no one I had ever been around. We cut our teeth on *The Graduate, Dr. Zhivago,* and *Easy Rider.* Cameron introduced me to the intriguing drawings of M.C. Escher, and I introduced him to the avant-garde poetry of Rod McKuen.

As intelligent as Cameron was, he had not been a very conscientious student his first two years of college. He realized it was time to settle down and get serious about a career. With the Vietnam War in the background and the draft looming, many playboys became scholars. In 1966, flunking out of college was a surefire way to get a personal invitation to Vietnam and that invite did not come with an RSVP. Since Cameron had always marched to a different drummer, he had aptly selected psychology as his major and, once into it, found an ardor and affinity for it. With his hypersensitivity to the world and the people in it, I was not surprised. We spent many afternoons in the cavernous Briarmore library dissecting the psychoanalytical works of Freud, Jung, and Adler.

Dr. and Mrs. Taylor were as special as Cameron, and we fell in love as quickly as Cameron and I had. Both sets of parents were, of course, surprised we had actually liked each other but were equally delighted. Matchmaking parents normally produced dire results.

Cameron and I were both passionate in our personalities and beliefs but not confrontational, so we seldom argued. Being unconditionally star-struck, I found everything Cameron did interesting and fascinating. I did not lose myself—not at all. I was still feisty as all get-out. But our basic personalities suited each other and the next few months waltzed by filled with Greek formals, house parties on the Gulf of Mexico, and the annual steak fry at a sorority sister's farm outside of Birmingham. I like to think I taught Cameron to be zany and a little giddy and to generally relish the moment. He taught me that the most special kind of love was one based on admiration and respect.

By September, Cameron gave me his fraternity pin to wear, which signified we were officially an exclusive couple. Even though it was three years off, we soon began to discuss marriage after my graduation as though it were a given. I even started a hope chest filled with things a bride might need for her first home. My mother and I found a beat-up cedar chest in a junk shop, and together we stained it a red-toned mahogany and needlepointed a beautiful floral tapestry for the top. It was gradually filled with my first pieces of china and silver, *The Joy of Cooking*, *Gone with the Wind* (one of my favorite novels), and some lovely damask hand towels procured from a linen shop in Birmingham's Mountain Brook Village. A silver letter opener engraved with a T was added after an antique shopping spree with my mother. Being a supreme optimist, I even added my favorite children's book *The Secret Garden*. I had accumulated a three-inch notebook filled with colored magazine pictures of chiffon and lace wedding gowns, mile-high, frosted cakes, and lavish floral arrangements.

Cameron seemed fine with all of this. He even threw in his favorite childhood book *Robinson Crusoe* in case our first child should be a boy, which as far as I was concerned was out of the question. After seeing *Dr. Zhivago*, I decided we should name our first child Lara, so of course, our firstborn had to be a girl. As I told Cameron, "I just can't see a boy going around with the name Lara." As far as I knew, Cameron had completely forgotten marriage was not in his future.

2

My assumption that Cameron was sexually experienced proved to be correct. Early in our relationship, after the long, lingering kisses led to quickened, breathless kisses, then further explorations, I reacted unlike, I am quite positive, most of his other previous girlfriends. Taken aback, he asked, "What's wrong?"

I took a deep breath. "I've been dreading this, but we have to talk."

Seeing my obvious distress, Cameron gently took my hand and said, "It's okay, Elisabeth, you can talk to me."

In the back of my mind, I knew what I was going to say would sound absolutely crazy, and I might lose the best-looking, wittiest boyfriend I had ever had, but I plowed ahead. "For some odd reason unknown even to me, at twelve years of age I decided I wanted to be a virgin when I walked down the aisle to be married. I want my white satin wedding dress to actually mean something. I do appreciate the fact that I was twelve years old and had no hormones. I appreciate that fact even more since I met you, but if I am nothing, I am loyal and tenacious even to an ideal. The really crazy thing is this has nothing to do with right or wrong. It is not some moral dogma that I was blindly indoctrinated in as a youth. It is just an ideal I believe in. I guess I have read too many Jane Austen novels."

As I had begun talking, I had moved back to give myself more space in order to get the words out. Cameron's crystal eyes got very soft, and he just sat there for a moment as he processed what I am sure he thought to be insanity. Then he lightly smiled and gently pulled me close to him. "Elisabeth, we can do this."

"We can?" My voice was a whisper.

"It's true. I have only known you for a short while, but I already know you are passionate and loyal and an oversized dreamer. This means a great deal to you. If you compromised now, you would always regret it on some level. I won't be the one to let you do that." Laughing he said, "I'm not having that on my conscience," and the tension was broken. "We can wait."

To this day I do not know how we did it, but we did. Cameron was one of the most disciplined men I had ever met. When I wanted to say to heck with it and have sex, he would say, "You don't really mean it. I know you and you would regret it." When Cameron broke up with me, it was the thing that saved me. Cameron left, but I walked away with my virginity. Some would call it crazy, but at the time it was my sanity.

The change in Cameron began after he graduated from Briarmore and went to a university two hours away to get his master's degree in psychology. The psychology department had more than its fair share of avant-garde individuals, and I think Cameron finally found a place where he felt at home. He grew his blond hair long and traded in his turtlenecks and cowboy boots for the tattered tee shirts and bare feet of a hippie. It was not that I was against individuality or free-thinking, but I just did not think you had to rebel to do it. Besides, I had far too much of an affinity for my Weejun loafers to exchange them for bare feet.

Being at two different schools did not help matters. We did not argue because that was not our modus operandi, but for the first time we began to disagree. The tension was palpable. When it came to unpleasantries, I was like my father and became an ostrich with my head stuck in the sand. While my head was in the sand, I could not see or hear, but I could not breathe, either.

11

We limped along until finally the day came when I had to come up for air, and in the kindest and gentlest of ways, Cameron told me he really did not believe in marriage and thought it would be best if we broke up. This took place the day after my graduation from Briarmore. Though I should not have been the least bit surprised at this turn of events, I was utterly devastated. I had stayed at school to finish packing and immediately called my mother and said between crying jags, "What on earth am I supposed to do with a hope chest?"

Shirley, my roommate who had the biggest laugh you had ever heard—surpassed only by her big heart—caught me in the throes of dismembering a favorite stuffed panda bear Cameron had given me. For the only time in our four years of rooming together, she berated me. "Stop that this instant. It is not that bear's fault Cameron broke up with you. Besides, one day you will regret tearing that poor panda to shreds." Then she took me in her arms as I sobbed with anger and hurt. Shirley, with her huge heart, put the stuffing back in the poor bear and sewed him up. I kept that panda to remind me that hurt and pain eventually pass. It was years later before I was to find out that was not always true.

In all fairness, Cameron Taylor had warned me on our first date about his disbelief in marriage, but at that juncture in my life I was under the mistaken assumption I controlled my world. Being independent and stubborn, I believed I could coerce people into doing my bidding. Cameron was my first lesson in reality that the world spins undauntedly on its axis and often leaves a trail of heartbreak behind.

My parents loved Cameron, and they were heartbroken for me. They always had an uncanny wisdom about when to keep silent, so when I returned home they allowed me to barricade myself in my bedroom and wallow in self-pity. The whole household bribed me by cooking my favorite foods, and though my heart was broken, I could not resist. At the end of the week, I did what I always did—I made a plan. My mother said I had been a planner and list-maker since the first day of kindergarten when I came home armed with a list of supplies needed by five-year-olds. Accompanying my mother to the store, I checked off each item with a big red crayon. I had been making plans and lists ever since.

My childhood friend Mary Kate had gotten a teaching job in Atlanta and needed a roommate. Since I had just lost my potential husband, I was a perfect candidate. By the end of July, I had ensconced myself in an apartment in Atlanta with Mary Kate and found a job teaching first grade.

3

Even though I was truly heartbroken, my innate optimism kicked into gear, and I began to look forward to getting back into the dating game. Mary Kate and I had heard that Atlanta was the single person's heaven, but it did not take long for that bit of hearsay to be proven wrong. My first foray into the dating world was with a football player I met at the Brave-Falcon Bar on Cheshire Bridge Road, a favorite Atlanta hot spot for singles. Billy Joe had been raised on a farm in a small town in Georgia and played right tackle at a nearby college. It seemed Billy Joe was having trouble passing English, and one night after a few dates, he asked me if I would help him critique a magazine article for his English class. The article was on sports, and I whipped out a one-page critique, thinking this would give him some pointers to go on. A few weeks later, I asked him how his critique turned out. "The professor gave it back to me and said there was no way I could have written it," he said.

"Billy Joe, you did change the handwriting, didn't you?" I asked. At this point, I decided Billy Joe probably was not the ideal mate for me. As I told Mary Kate, "Remind me never to date anyone whose neck size is bigger than my waist."

I met Dan in the parking lot of our apartment building one afternoon as I was coming home from school. He and his girlfriend had just broken up, and he had come to reclaim some of his things. Dan was very outgoing and loads of fun. He was a little on the juvenile side, but unfortunately, I was finding that to be rather common in the twenty-something male species. We had three really fun dates, and suddenly I did not hear from him for over a week. It was then I made a huge error in judgment and broke a cardinal rule that Southern parents beat into their Southern daughters: I called Dan on the telephone. As I was growing up, my parents had threatened me within an inch of my life if I ever even thought about calling a boy on the phone. It just was not done by respectable girls. Since I valued my young life, I had not until now broken this ironclad rule. I was going to give it four rings, and when Dan answered on the fourth ring, he sounded a little breathless. "Hi," I said, "this is Elisabeth. What are you doing?"

He stammered a little bit and then said, "You're not going to believe this, but I am in a very compromising position." Even I knew that was code for having sex. "My girlfriend and I got back together, and we are celebrating."

With a very red face, I immediately got off the phone. I was thinking to myself that this would have been one of those times when lying would have been perfectly acceptable, even preferable. As I told Mary Kate, "Remind me never to date a guy who will not lie to one girl while he is in the act of having sex with another girl."

Next came Malcolm. I had gone out with some teachers from school, and he was a friend of one of their husbands. Malcolm had his MBA and was very good-looking and intelligent. We dated for a month, and I thought things were going well when suddenly he quit calling. Sure enough, at school my friend told me Malcolm had gone back to an ex-girlfriend. All I could think was, thank goodness, I had not called him in the act of celebrating this momentous event. I asked Mary Kate, "What is it with ex-girlfriends? Do I have a sign around my neck—date Elisabeth Sterling and you will get your ex-girlfriend back?"

Soon I met James at a party a friend threw in our apartment building. More than good-looking, he was teddy bear cute and an unapologetic flirt, so we started dating. James was a transplant from the North, who had graduated from Penn State and had a very good job with IBM. Right before I left Atlanta to go home for the Christmas holidays, he told me he had gotten tickets through work to the Orange Bowl, where Penn State and Missouri were playing, and asked if I wanted to go with him. New Year's Eve in Miami sounded like great fun, so I readily accepted. Since I grew up in the Florida Panhandle, I offered for him to stay at my house en route, and James graciously accepted. Exactly three days before he was to arrive at my house, James called to tell me there had been a change of plans, and he was not going to be able to take me to the Orange Bowl. In my mind, the word "ex-girlfriend" reared its ugly head, but I was gracious to James about it all. I called Mary Kate. "I'm an ex-girlfriend. Do you see Cameron Taylor beating down my door? Where's the justice in all this?" I asked her.

"Elisabeth, it seems with you and dating right now justice is taking a break," Mary Kate answered.

But the proverbial straw that broke the camel's back came in January with a blind date. Stu was a friend of a friend's friend, so that was the first sign I was handed into the territory called desperation. It was so bad it does not deserve repeating, but suffice it to say, it involved an excessively inebriated male and a furtive cab ride home.

It was at this juncture I decided to enter the realm of old maids. Since my flair for histrionics was without equal, I considered becoming a nun. Like I told Mary Kate, "Just think, you would never have to worry about what to wear and 'Bad Hair Day' would be a thing of the past."

But Mary Kate quickly dissuaded me of this ingenious idea. "Elisabeth," she said, "you are not one for the confines of a convent. You're entirely too feisty. Quite frankly, you make Maria in *The Sound of Music* look like Mother Superior. Besides, you are not even Catholic." That left the world of an old maid. It was at this point I applied to graduate school since I was now a confirmed spinster and would need to support myself for the rest of my life. As I saw it, this world was fine with me as long as the male species was not in any form or fashion a part of it.

4

My graduate plans were all neatly packaged when my colleague Jane waylaid me in the teacher's lounge on a Monday morning in February. Jane was a second year teacher and had been a godsend to me. Being a neophyte, I was totally unprepared for a classroom full of breathing, squirming six-year-olds. "All teaching is baptism by fire," Jane assured me and with her helpful tips and guidance I had settled into the world of first graders with great relish.

"Elisabeth, I have been looking for you. I have a huge favor to ask." For about six months now, Jane had been dating Tom, a Second Lieutenant stationed at Fort Benning in Columbus, Georgia. From all outward indications, they were madly in love and headed toward blissful matrimony. I really liked Tom. He was cute in a stuffed animal kind of way with personality to spare. Jane and Tom made a very compatible couple. "Tom is coming this weekend and bringing one of his best buddies from base. Will you please, please go on a blind date with his friend?"

Needless to say, hearing "blind" and "date" in the same sentence struck unadulterated terror in my heart. "Jane, my last blind date is a major factor in my recent decision to almost enter a convent."

"That bad, uh?"

"Stu had graduated from Georgia Tech. I always thought it took brains to get into Georgia Tech, but apparently I was mistaken. He took me to a party at a friend's apartment and, before I knew it, proceeded to get knee-walkin' drunk. Ole Stu was standing in a corner drooling with his head wobbling like a bobbing apple. The girl I was talking to spied him and inquired if I knew who his date was. I replied I had absolutely no idea—had never seen him before. She said, 'Man, I feel sorry for that girl.' To which I replied with the utmost sincerity, 'So do I.' I managed to sneak out of the apartment and call a cab before anyone found out I was the poor date. It was a most humiliating experience."

"Look, Elisabeth, I'm not asking you to marry this guy. Just go on one date. Tom told me he was a West Point graduate. How bad can that be?" To this day, I have no idea why I agreed to break my vow and go on the date. My grandmother would have called it divine intervention.

When I arrived at Jane's that Friday night, I could not believe it when I met my blind date. Being an incurable romantic, it was no surprise the minute I saw the movie *Camelot*, I was lost. Guinevere got it all wrong. King Arthur's strength was like an anchor while at the same time being gentle and sensual. Lancelot, loyal as he was, seemed too feckless and over the top. Here I was, a misplaced denizen of Camelot, and standing in front of me was a knight in shining armor. He even had an enchanted name and a mass of silky black hair. His name was Kincaid. I do not know what I fell in love with first—that mane of magnificent hair or his magical name.

We all went to dinner at a steak house Jane had been dying to try. The food was delicious, the conversation witty and lively. It was turning into one of those rare evenings when the poet Robert Browning would say *all's right with the world*. Kincaid had a humorous, dry wit, which delighted me, but there was a pronounced seriousness about him that I sensed came from somewhere deep within his being. Discreetly studying him, I could not imagine Kincaid ever being an awkward twelve-year-old, who like O'Neal Jones in junior high would try to knock a book out of my lap or like Adam Presley who told me I sang like a frog in Mrs. Hendrick's music class. When I complained to my mother, she said, "O'Neal Jones likes you and you do sing like a frog."

When we got back to Jane's apartment, Jane and Tom headed to the bedroom. Kincaid grabbed a beer, poured me a glass of wine, and we sat down on the sofa. I sensed neither one of us wanted the evening to end. "Well, Elisabeth," Kincaid said, "you strike me as a very entertaining person. Why don't you tell me your life story?"

"Really?" I asked.

"Really," Kincaid said, "tell me about your childhood." Kincaid seemed very sincere, and I loved to talk, so I began to regale him about my life thus far.

5

"My childhood was a magical time," I said to Kincaid as we settled down to talk. "I was born in Hillston, Florida. My youth was filled with unleased freedom—playing in the city park, riding my bike throughout the town, visiting with neighbors. I'm very close to my parents."

"Hillston must be really small. I've never even heard of it. Tell me about your parents and this town I've never heard of," Kincaid said.

Hillston is in the Florida Panhandle, 55 miles from the sugar white sands and crystal azure waters of the Gulf of Mexico. It is a town of roughly 5000 population, and as far as I knew, everyone was my neighbor. My father, Lawson Sterling, was a lawyer who specialized in estate law and wills but who in actuality practiced just about anything that had to do with legal matters in our rural town. My father was tall and lanky with aquiline features and graying at his dark-haired temples. He wore wire-rimmed glasses perched on his sharp nose, and I fancied him to be a modern-day Atticus Finch. My father even had Atticus' calm manner and methodical approach to life, and I thought enveloped more wisdom than Mr. Lucas, the ancient owl that lived in the woods at the end of our street. I named the owl in honor of the real-life Mr. Lucas, who when I was a small girl, sat in the creaky rocker on the wooden porch of Mr. Jones' general store and spat out adages the whole day long. One time Mr. Lucas told me if I did not stop opening my bobby pins with my front teeth I was going to be "buck-teethed" for the rest of my life. Dr. Fields, my dentist, assured me that was not the case but, at best, putting filthy bobby pins in my mouth was not sanitary. The sanitary part did not bother me one whit but the buck-teeth sure did, and for some inexplicable reason, wizened Mr. Lucas seemed more credible than Dr. Fields, so I ceased my bobby pin habit immediately. Mr. Lucas dropped dead suddenly at age 99 in the middle of spouting one of his pearls of wisdom. I, for one, thought it was a great way to go. My mother said, "You would. You always have to have the last word."

My mother, Louise Stewart Sterling, was a housewife and the personification of efficiency. Growing up, it would not have surprised me in the least to walk in our house one day and see her vacuuming while wearing high heels and pearls like the woman in the Hoover vacuum cleaner ads. She was tall and thin with ash-blonde hair and gray-blue eyes, which I thought an interesting contrast to my father's smoky-dark hair and chocolate-brown eyes. My mother may have looked wispy with her lean frame and fair aura but that was an illusion. She was as strong as any woman I knew and, most decidedly, as intelligent. Louise was a charter member of the Junior Service League as well as active in the Hillston Garden Club, Woman's Club, and one book club. It was a good thing my mother, at least, had a green thumb because she was a terrible cook. My family would have surely perished of starvation if it had not been for our cook, Queenie. We would have had to be sustained on the only two culinary dishes my mother had been able to master—watery ham and potato casserole and frozen fruit cocktail salad. Frozen fruit cocktail salad contained exactly two ingredients—three, if you count the juice in the can of fruit cocktail. Made out of cream cheese and canned fruit, it was frozen in a metal ice cube tray and your teeth got "freezer burn" when you bit into it. My mother actually had the audacity to submit the Frozen Fruit

Cocktail Salad recipe for the *Hillston Woman's Club Cookbook*. There is nothing like telling the whole world you are a bad cook.

"Elisabeth, your parents sound so interesting. Where did they meet?"

"They really are pretty wonderful," I said.

My father had gone to the University of Florida undergraduate school and continued there to study law. He met my mother the summer before his last year of law school. She had just finished her first year at Florida State College for Women in the days before it became coed and changed its name to Florida State University. They immediately fell in love, and seeing how attractive they each are years later, I could understand why. Mother left college after her sophomore year to marry my father that October. They moved to Hillston, where my father had hung his shingle in his father's law office. Ten months later, I came along. They named me Elisabeth Belle after both grandmothers. I have always loved that fact and that Elisabeth was spelled with an *s*. It seemed to make me special.

They had a scare when I was two. Mother was stricken with polio and rushed to Pensacola, Florida, where she was placed in an iron lung. At the time, polio patients were getting treatment at Warm Springs, Georgia, and my father got her admitted, where she made remarkable progress. In just three months, she was walking in the heated pool there. My grandparents kept me while my parents were at Warm Springs. Two months later, Mother came home for good. She only had to wear a brace on one leg for a while and, after a year, was walking normally and even dancing. Mother always said she was one of the lucky ones, and she kept that leg brace in the cedar chest in the hallway to remind herself how fortunate she had been.

It was obvious to everyone that my mother and father adored each other. Though she had not finished college, my

23

mother was my father's intellectual equal. They were both voracious readers, and lively conversations and debates about politics, religion, and the condition of the world were always flying around our living room. No one except me ever yelled in our household. Because both of my parents were strong-willed in their own quiet way, I know they must have argued, but they always did it behind their closed bedroom door.

"And then there's my brother, Stewart," I said wryly.

Kincaid laughed at the way I said it. "I'm an only child. I always wanted a brother so I would have someone to play football with."

Stewart came along when I was five, and it was years before I forgave him for interrupting my life. Whereas my appearance was light like my mother's, his was dark like my father's. As is often the case, even with identical parents, our personalities and temperaments were polar opposites. For most of my life, I found Stewart to be the bane of my existence. I truly believed he had been put on this earth to annoy, pester, and torture me, and he succeeded in doing all three with exceptional skill. In all fairness to Stewart, five years difference was not an acceptable age span for a younger brother. If we had been closer in age, I think we would have been formidable allies. The only time Stewart and I joined forces was when it was to our mutual benefit to be a united front. It was usually some trivial concern. Stewart hated peas and I hated carrots. My normally sane parents became lunatics when it came to their children and vegetables. So I hid Stewart's peas in my pockets, and he hid my carrots. Our parents were never the wiser, and neither Stewart nor I grew up with a vitamin deficiency.

My brother and I were taught impeccable manners in the Southern style. It was always "Yes, ma'am," "No, sir," "Please," "Thank you," and "May I?" Differences, within reason, were encouraged as was independence and free-thinking. However, you did not even think for one second of talking back to an elder. The only offense my father ever swatted my backside for was sassin,' and it happened on more than one occasion. As my mother was forever pointing out, I always had to have the last word. We could laugh with people but never at them. I still remember with distinct clarity the day Ella Sadler and I caught Ray Wilson and Will Smitherton making fun of a workman, who was sitting outside the chain link fence of our elementary school playground eating his lunch. We pelted Ray and Will with pine cones until they ran away and told the man we were sorry, but they were just dumb ole boys who didn't have a brain. The workman never looked up but just said, "You sure are nice little girls." My mother and grandmother never admitted it, but I inherited my feistiness from them. They were just quiet about it—an art I never mastered.

"I have to tell you about Queenie. She was such a special part of my childhood," I continued.

"I love her name," Kincaid said. "It's so Southern."

Queenie, who was oversized and buxom, was our cook and one of the loves of my youth. I imagine she was also my father's secret love as she cooked him fluffy biscuits, mouth-watering, crispy fried chicken, and homemade cherry pie with just the correct amount of tartness and sweetness. It always fascinated me to watch her cut strips of dough with precision, crisscross them on top of the plump cherries, and brush the top with egg white so it would come out of the oven a shiny golden brown. But Queenie was most renowned for her pound cake as it was the best for miles around. Strangely enough, I did not care for pound cake, but I absolutely relished the batter. I would sit up on our kitchen counter made of small terra cotta tiles and patiently wait watching the Sunbeam mixer go round and round while Queenie scraped the sides of the bowl with her wooden spatula. My patience would be rewarded as I licked every drop of gooey, golden batter off the beaters and out of the bowl until my nose was dripping with pound cake mix. Then Queenie would laugh and enfold me in her strong arms, and you could see where I left specks of yellow batter on her ebony skin. "You're a mess, Elisabeth Belle," she would say, and she meant that literally and figuratively. Then she would pat me on the bottom and say, "Get along, Sugah Pie. I got to get this cake in the oven for Mister Lawson."

As we did for all adults, Stewart and I said "Yes, ma'am" and "No, ma'am" to Queenie and thanked her for every single meal she ever cooked even if it was the liver and onion my mother insisted she serve once a month. Queenie's niece Tabitha came for a week visit one summer, and she and I played jacks and hopscotch and jumped rope all day long.

"As close as I am to my parents, in some ways I am even closer to my grandmother. My grandmother is one of the most remarkable women I have ever met," I said with pride.

"You have me again. I never knew any of my grandparents. What did you call her?" Kincaid asked.

Grandmother Reid, my father's mother, was the heroine of my life. Reid was her maiden name, and since she was a woman before her time, I always thought it appropriate we addressed her as such. Raised by an intelligent widowed aunt on a farm in Georgia, she had gone to a teacher's college in the northern part of the state. Because few women had obtained higher education at the turn of the century, she was rightly very proud of this accomplishment. One of my favorites among the pictures sitting on my desk is of my fresh-faced grandmother in a beautiful batiste lace frock with a large bow in the back of her dark brown hair. Holding her teaching diploma in her right hand, she is smiling broadly, and her look of accomplishment in that sepia photograph has always been an inspiration.

She met my grandfather while teaching in a one-room schoolhouse in rural Georgia. Lawson Sterling Sr. "swept her off her feet," as she used to tell me. As a young girl, I had a vivid image of my grandfather swatting my grandmother's feet with a broom. When she realized this, she immediately set me straight. As I grew, it did not take me long to realize no one would ever swat my grandmother with a broom if they wanted to live to see the sun rise the next day. My grandparents married in a quiet ceremony in her uncle's home, and three years later their only child, my father, was born. My Grandfather Sterling was a lawyer, and in 1930, they moved to the town of Hillston, which was in its infancy. My grandfather rose to county judge, and even after his retirement, everyone called him Judge Sterling. He died when I was only three, so my only remembrances are a deep, soft lap and a scratchy, white-whiskered beard. I spent many a night with my grandparents, who lived within walking distance from our house, and in the mornings at breakfast Granddaddy Sterling would kiss me and rub his white unshaven stubble on my cheeks until I would beg him to stop and run away laughing.

My grandmother was short and petite, but her stature belied her enormous inner strength. I spent many hours of my childhood with my Grandmother Reid and loved her with a complete and unequivocal adoration. She loved cards and taught me Canasta, Rook, and Hearts. She eschewed Bridge, which she deemed much too serious to be fun, and to Grandmother Reid, if life was not fun, it just was not worth fooling with. Board games were another favorite, and we spent countless hours engaged in a battle of wits of Checkers, Monopoly, and Chinese checkers. To this day, I can whip anybody in Chinese checkers, and I consider it a fitting tribute to Grandmother Reid. Her forte was her "quizzes." By age ten, I knew every state and its capitol. Except for South Dakotans, I was probably the only ten-year-old who was aware that Pierre was the capitol of South Dakota. She taught me the name and order of every book of the Bible, and I was always the victor in the Sunday School Bible drills at the First Methodist Church of Hillston. Our Sunday School teacher, Mr. Hall, would call out *Ezekiel* and all the other ten-year-olds would stare dumb-faced as I flipped right to it. Mr. Hall finally asked me to sit out a few rounds so the other kids would have a chance. I was not to blame for this precociousness. It was all Grandmother Reid's fault. It was also Grandmother Reid's fault I was so competitive. To this day, I hate to lose. She never let me win but made me earn a victory in my own right. It was only natural I would love my Grandmother Reid so completely. I was a ready student and the center of her universe. Having stellar health and an amazing mind, she was still active in all her clubs and church work, but when I was around nothing else was important. We relished each other's company.

"I probably should stop now," I said. "I could talk forever about my family. It's embarrassing."

"Just a little longer, Elisabeth. It's not even midnight yet," Kincaid said with a smile. "Tell me more about your family. You said they loved to read. What about vacations?" Surprisingly, Kincaid really did seem interested in my life.

Because of my parents' influence, I began a life-long love affair with books from the moment I learned to decipher the written word in Mrs. Talbot's first grade class. From children's readers I graduated to the series of historical "We Were There" books—I was at the Alamo, on the Lewis and Clark expedition, and at the construction of the Erie Canal. Next I became Nancy Drew. It was not too big a stretch in my mind as she was also blonde and her father a lawyer. By age eleven, I had read every Nancy Drew mystery Carolyn Keene had authored. By high school, my parents had me reading the classics, and it did not take long for me to become the frivolous Daisy Buchannan or the long-suffering Jane Eyre.

We were the type of family that settled down together in the oak-paneled den to watch our favorite television shows on the black and white RCA. With a complete absence of musical ability, we belted out our favorite tunes on *Your Hit Parade* like we were The Supremes. Stewart became the rugged cowboys of *Bonanza*, whereas I was entranced by the mysteriously masked, swashbuckling Zorro. My parents fancied themselves Alice and Ralph Kramden on *The Honeymooners* when in truth nothing could be further from reality. My father and I loved to watch *Gunsmoke* together. Secretly, I think my rather straitlaced father envisioned himself a rough-hewn U.S. Marshal. I had a special affinity for Miss Kitty, who seemed so glamorous and worldly with all those feathers flying everywhere. Turned out she was, indeed, both of those things.

Every summer my family piled into my mother's black Buick and headed the 55 miles to the white sands and blue-green waters of the Gulf of Mexico. We always stayed at Grantham's Cottages in Panama City Beach. The cottages had black and white linoleum floors and window air conditioning units that always sounded like they were blowing out their last gasp of cold air. My father would walk Stewart and me down to the local grocery store where we would each purchase a brightly colored raft and an ice cream bar. I had a love for Dreamsicles, and to this day, I can close my eyes and still taste the frozen burst of orange sherbet and vanilla ice cream on my tongue. My father would find a gray concrete building block and anchor our rafts in the warm gulf where we would lazily float as the salty water lapped against our browning skin. When mother decided we were getting too much sun, she would drag us underneath the large, striped umbrella dug into the grainy sand. For the next few hours, I would become Nancy Drew as I solved the mystery of *The Hidden Staircase* or *The Secret in the Old Attic*. We feasted on fried shrimp, red snapper, and hushpuppies. At night, I would lay my head on my father's lap as he rocked in the old wooden swing on the patio. Our gaily colored swimsuits strung across the clothesline would slowly flap in the soft summer breeze, and I would fall asleep to the gentle creaking of the swing and the mesmerizing roar of the ocean.

I was a child of polar dichotomies. I could be as content snuggled in our den love seat with a Nancy Drew mystery as I could be running wild with the neighborhood kids in the woods at the end of our street. I loved to dress up in my Buster Brown pumps and frilly, ruffled dresses my mother and grandmother created as much as I loved donning cut-offs and playing basketball and tag football with the boys in the Hillston City Park. I was impulsive and overly dramatic, but if something interested me, I could focus on it for hours. Short and petite like my Grandmother Reid, I had inherited her stubbornness and independence to boot. I believe my mother spent my entire youth trying to figure me out. She never quite knew what I was going to come up with next. While my mother was shaking her head in dismay, my father just laughed and kicked back in his armchair to read the paper.

Stewart and I learned at an early age that our father was the hub of the household. We were never coddled, and it was always our fault, which was a very good reason to steer away from trouble. I grew up surrounded on all sides feeling loved, accepted, and most important of all, safe.

6

At this point, Kincaid and I realized it was past midnight, and I had been talking for over an hour. I could not fathom that anyone would find my childhood interesting, but Kincaid seemed to hang on every word. Embarrassed I said, "Sorry, I got a little carried away. I should have let you talk first."

"My childhood was much shorter," Kincaid said with a mischievous grin.

When Kincaid walked me to my car, I turned around and said, "If you are planning on asking me out for a second date, I better warn you. I'm in love with Robert Redford."

"In that case, Elisabeth Belle, I'm the man for you. I love a good challenge." With that, Kincaid Patterson gave me a military salute and, in perfect gentlemanly fashion, opened the car door for me.

The ringing telephone woke me up Saturday morning. "Hello, Eliza. Would you have dinner with me this evening?" I heard Kincaid Patterson saying on the other end.

"Eliza?"

"Ever since I saw *My Fair Lady*, I have had a thing for Eliza Doolittle."

"You mean the part where the professor orders her around like a male chauvinistic pig?"

"It's Eliza herself. I love her spunk. Plus, I'm attracted to her."

"Ninety per cent of the men in America have a Natalie Wood pinup, and you have a pinup of Eliza Doolittle. Have you considered therapy?"

"Would you please have dinner with me this evening?"

"Yes I will, Professor Higgins, but I'm not bringing you your bedroom slippers."

Kincaid took me to an Italian restaurant located in the Buckhead section of Atlanta. It was perfect with a warm, romantic ambience and delicious, spicy food. I could not believe that I had just met Kincaid the night before as he was so comfortable to be with, like an old friend I had not seen in a while. There was none of the awkwardness usually associated with first dates. As I sat gazing at Kincaid across the table, I was still in awe of his gorgeous mane of dark hair. His eyes were so dark they seemed almost black, and they had such depth it was as though you were looking into a window of his soul. He was six feet tall with the toned physique of a soldier. There was a calmness about him that was soothing but a sensuality that was unsettling. Kincaid was one of those men that had effortless sex appeal. Even if he had taken the vows of a monk, women would have taken notice when he walked by. As my roommate Mary Kate would so picturesquely say, "That man exudes testosterone."

If there had been an outside observer, the differences in the man and woman seated at this table would be quite apparent. I was a petite 5 feet 2 inches with blonde hair and blue eyes. Kincaid was a steady rock, I was a flitting butterfly. My nature was inquisitive to a fault, and I was known to babble to fill in silences. Kincaid, on the other hand, would find purpose in silence. Because of my Southern upbringing, I was unctuously polite and kind yet possessed an innate sarcasm. As I had noted on the first date, Kincaid had that dry wit that would strike you with subtle hilarity.

Not wanting the night to end, after dinner Kincaid suggested we go back to Jane's to have a last drink before he took me home. "But this time I'm not doing all the talking," I said. "I want to hear about your life." After we settled on the sofa with our drinks, I could tell Kincaid was not thrilled about talking about himself, but in my stubborn way I insisted. "It is only fair," I pointed out. "I talked nonstop for over an hour last night." Reluctantly, Kincaid began to tell me his story.

7

As Kincaid began talking, I could sense in his words the gravity with which he lived life. His quick wit was tempered by a deep seriousness. "I was born in Pascagoula, Mississippi," Kincaid said. "My father, Barrett Patterson, was a very intelligent man. His greatest desire was to go to college, but the summer after his high school graduation, his father died from a massive heart attack. My father had to go into the shrimping business to support his family."

"Not being able to go to college must have been a huge disappointment to him. Then he had the shock of losing his father so young," I said.

"I know, it had to be an extremely difficult time, but I never heard him complain about it. He met my mother when she came to Pascagoula to live with her cousin. She was working in a dress shop downtown. I was born not long after they married."

As Kincaid continued to tell me about his father, I could sense how close they had been. Kincaid's father loved to read and fostered a devotion to literature in his son. They spent hours sharing books. Kincaid was a natural athlete, and his father was a constant presence on the sidelines. During the summer, Kincaid worked along with the men on his father's shrimping boat, relishing the camaraderie of the shrimpers, the feel of the rolling sea beneath him, and the spray of the salt air on his face.

"When I was twelve, there was a picture of a local boy in the newspaper who had gotten an appointment to West Point. You should have seen the look of pride on my father's face when he saw that picture. I decided right then I would go to the military academy," Kincaid said earnestly. From that moment on, Kincaid became totally focused on his goal, and his father encouraged him every step of the way. Kincaid researched all the requirements—he kept his grades up, worked hard at his chosen sport of football, and stayed out of trouble.

When Kincaid was fifteen, his father died of a heart attack while out on his shrimp boat. Barrett's best friend Samson was the one to tell Kincaid. Barrett Patterson was a beloved man, and there was not a dry eye at his memorial. Big, burly shrimpers broke down and wept. They all knew they had lost one of God's finest. It was the greatest tragedy that could befall Kincaid, and the only thing that kept him going was his inalienable desire to get into West Point for his father. There were four people that saved him in this period of his life: Kincaid's best friend, Robbie Williams, Robbie's parents, Mr. and Mrs. Williams, who treated Kincaid like their own son, and Samson, who was like a surrogate father.

Kincaid got the appointment to West Point where he excelled. He loved military life. The structure and the rigorous studies suited his personality and natural acumen. After graduation, he went into military intelligence. He spent a year in school for training and then was sent to Fort Benning, where he had been stationed since last May. As Kincaid was talking, even though we had just met, I could immediately sense he was an exemplary officer. Besides his obvious intelligence, he exuded quiet confidence and strong self-discipline.

"Don't you require a nomination from a United States Congressman to get in West Point?" I asked. "How did you manage that?"

"It's a very long story," he replied, "and an age-old one at that."

"I'm actually a very good listener," I said.

Not long after Barrett's death, Samson told Kincaid about a plan Barrett had to help Kincaid acquire a congressional nomination for West Point. In high school, Barrett had been in love with a beautiful and intelligent girl by the name of Delores Richardson. They had met in English class over their mutual passion for books and fallen deeply in love. Mr. Richardson was president of the local bank, and when he found out about the romance, he was livid. He had no intention of allowing his only daughter to consort with a shrimper's son.

When Mr. Richardson confronted Delores and demanded she end the liaison, Delores was defiant for one of the rare times in her life and refused. Like most of the shrimpers in Pascagoula, Barrett's father borrowed money from the bank to get him through the season. He always paid it back like clockwork. Mr. Richardson called Mr. Patterson to his office and threatened to withhold the loan if he did not get his son to end the relationship. Barrett had no choice. Delores was painfully hurt and went off to Ole Miss that summer.

Delores graduated from Ole Miss and married the wealthy son of a banker from Jackson, Mississippi. Her husband immediately got into politics and eventually was elected to the U.S. House of Representatives from his district with the help of his father's power and money. Kincaid had seen an attractive woman standing away from the crowd at his father's funeral. It was obvious by her composure and dress that she was wealthy. There was a look on her face of longing and sorrow that Kincaid could not put out of his mind. Barrett had no communication with Delores all these years, but his plan was to contact her and ask for her help with Kincaid's nomination to West Point.

The next year Kincaid wrote a letter to Delores asking for a meeting. She consented, and they met in a restaurant in Jackson. Kincaid was struck by her gentility and by what he sensed was a deep, underlying sorrow. She could not have been any more gracious and promised Kincaid she would get the nomination for him. Delores was as good as her word, and his senior year in high school the nomination came from her husband's office.

"That took a lot of courage, Kincaid. What kind of man was her husband?" I asked.

"From what Samson had heard, a complete cad. Of course, Delores could not confide in a teenage boy, but it was obvious she still cared deeply for my father. I think my nomination was her last gift to him."

"That is unfortunate. Delores sounds like a lovely individual who got a rotten deal in life."

"I don't mean this unkindly, Elisabeth, but in your magical world you probably have no idea of the number of people who get rotten deals in life." I was not upset because I knew it was true. My life had been immensely blessed.

I also found out that along with his love of books, like me, Kincaid was a movie aficionado. He loved *MASH*, which we had both just seen, *The Graduate*, *Cool Hand Luke*, *Barefoot in the Park*, and *Dr. Zhivago*. Unlike me, music was a passion. "You do know who the Beatles are?" he teasingly asked me.

"Okay, wise guy, I also know who Elvis Presley is."

"What a relief!"

"And I have a favorite song, I'll have you know— *Unchained Melody*."

"That doesn't surprise me a bit."

"Of course, it doesn't. It is one of the most romantic songs ever written, and I am an incurable romantic."

It was obvious Kincaid was omitting a part of his childhood. He had barely mentioned his mother. "What about your mother?" I finally asked.

37

Kincaid got very still, and I could see his jaw moving with tension. "My mother is not a part of my life. I have not had any communication with her in a long time and that will never change. One thing you will have to learn, Elisabeth, is that I do not ever talk about my mother." Kincaid said it with such ferocious finality that even I, with my abundantly inquisitive nature, knew to keep my silence. Kincaid's mother would remain a mysterious figure hidden in the shadows of his childhood.

Then Kincaid said, "Our childhoods could not have been any more different. Yours is like a fairy tale. Listening to you talk about your youth, I had the same feeling as when my father read to me the stories of King Arthur and his Knights of the Round Table."

I felt my heart do a complete somersault. "You like *Camelot*?" I asked.

"Are you kidding? After my father read me those stories, for the next year, I was King Arthur."

"Not Lancelot, but King Arthur?"

"Definitely King Arthur," Kincaid said.

"So you knew Guinevere got it wrong."

"Guinevere definitely got it wrong."

8

For the next few weekends, Tom and Kincaid drove the two hours from Columbus to Atlanta. Kincaid and I talked on the telephone every day, and there was no doubt we were falling in love with each other. We had our first argument about a month after we met. One night Kincaid was over an hour late calling at our usual time, and in my usual impatient way, I was having a full-blown hissy fit by the time the phone finally rang. Not even giving Kincaid time for an explanation, I launched into full attack mode. Kincaid did the most amazing thing, which was absolutely nothing. He did not get defensive, he did not get angry—he just patiently waited for my unreasonable tirade to cease.

"Are you through?" he asked. "Would you like to know why I was late calling?"

"Yes, I would," I said, much calmer now. His calm demeanor had made me realize how immature I was acting.

"Major Stanford called a meeting. We had an emergency on base, but everything is fine now."

"Oh, Kincaid, I'm sorry. I totally overreacted. I am afraid I have the patience of a gnat. Also, you need to know, I have a very low tolerance for suffering. I could never be a martyr. Martyrs get on my last nerve—except maybe Joan of Arc. I'm willing to give Joan of Arc a pass."

"Elisabeth Belle," he said laughing, "I imagine life with you could be most entertaining."

Kincaid called the next night and said, "Elisabeth, I can't get off this weekend. Could you drive here? This may come as a shock to you, but the military does not have the same hours and holidays as the educational system."

"Quit complaining, Kincaid. You get free aspirin, for goodness sake, and I'll be glad to come to you." Knowing this day was soon coming, I took a deep breath and said, "There is one little fact I need to enlighten you."

"Shoot, I'm all ears."

Plunging ahead before I lost my nerve, I said, "Well, it's like this. I am—well, you see, I have never...." I felt like an inexperienced sixteen-year-old, which in theory is what I was. There was a long pause.

"Are you still there?" Kincaid asked.

"Oh for Pete's sake, Kincaid, I'm a virgin." There was a long silence. Finally I asked, "Are you still there?"

Then Kincaid said, "You sure don't look like a virgin."

I could not help it. I laughed until tears were streaming down my face. "I just thought I should give you fair warning."

Through the phone, I could hear Kincaid laughing. "Come down here next weekend, Elisabeth. I'm sure we can work around this little revelation."

When I hung up the phone, I went into the kitchen where Mary Kate was munching on a leaf of lettuce. She had just met Bruce, who seemed like a good marriage possibility, and was determined to lose five pounds. Quite frankly, Bruce did not impress me, but Mary Jane had her eyes set on matrimony, so I kept my mouth shut. "Do I look like a virgin?" I asked her.

"No," she deadpanned, "your boobs are too big."

Jane and I drove to Fort Benning for the weekend. To keep from thinking about sex, Kincaid and I played Chinese checkers and Scrabble. Thanks to Grandmother Reid's tutelage, I clobbered him in Chinese checkers. Kincaid was just getting an inkling of my very competitive nature. When I beat him in

Scrabble with the word *sex*, that did it, plus I got extra points for using the *x*. He turned the game board upside down and held me down and tickled me until I pled for mercy. Just to show what a good sport I was, I picked up every single Scrabble tile.

I will have to admit Kincaid never got the chastity belt bit, but one beautiful August evening exactly six months from the night I regaled him with my life story, instead of walking down the halls of the University of Georgia, I was walking down the aisle of the First Methodist Church of Hillston, clad in a luminous white satin wedding gown that actually meant something. For punctuated legitimacy, my dream gown had been hand-beaded by Grandmother Reid's closest friend, Mrs. Lee. It was also my twenty-third birthday.

Our reception was a festive affair at the Hillston Country Club with all the usual trimmings of yellow and white roses, a sugar-frosted, tiered cake, spicy chicken wings, and sparkling champagne. We exited to a shower of rice and a trail of tin cans tied to Kincaid's red Ford Fairlane. We made it exactly thirty minutes out of town to the first motel we came to—a Travel Lodge with the sleepy bear logo.

It was a good thing I did not know what I had been missing all those years, or I would never have been a twenty-three-year-old virgin. I asked mischievously, "Can we do this again?" Kincaid laughed and tousled my mussed hair as he said, "For the rest of our lives, Elisabeth Belle."

From the first, we were magically attuned both physically and emotionally. It was no surprise to me that Kincaid was sexually experienced. I had long faced the fact I was drawn to sensual men like a moth drawn to light. We literally could not get enough of each other. Our lovemaking was in turn gentle, passionate, playful, lingering. Kincaid teased me, "You are an incredibly fast learner, Eliza."

41

"Well, if you had twenty-three years of sexual frustration, wouldn't you learn fast?" Kincaid just laughed and pulled me to him covering my mouth with his.

We spent our honeymoon in the sleepy fishing village of Destin, Florida. It was a wise decision not to waste money on some exotic destination since we barely left our motel room. We mostly just saw the sandy beige walls of our room and the muted colors of the seascape prints hanging on the walls. I finally moved the pictures around for a little variety since I could not move the bed.

While in Destin, we talked about our dreams and plans for the future. We both wanted a family, and naively, I assured Kincaid I was up for all the moves and upheavals of an Army wife. He told me the reason he wanted to go to the Gulf of Mexico for our honeymoon was that he loved my stories of our family vacations on the beach. "You know it is all your fault I am not going to be an old maid," I told him.

"You would have been a terrible old maid, Elisabeth."

"Come to think of it, it probably wasn't one of my better ideas."

I told him I knew after our first argument that I was going to marry him if he happened to ask me. "Why after our first argument?" Kincaid asked.

"I knew I needed someone who could keep their mouth shut when I got angry. My father did that to me, and it always calmed me down."

"Have you forgiven me for proposing to you in front of the entire U.S. Army?"

"Actually, quite the contrary. When you get really angry at me, you can't deny asking me to marry you. I have all those witnesses."

"The truth is I didn't trust myself to be alone with you. That white wedding dress might have had to be pink."

"A pink wedding dress—what a novel idea. Just announce to the world you have already had sex."

Kincaid had proposed to me the first week of June right after I had finished teaching for the school year. His best friends at Fort Benning were Karen and Curt Phillips, and I had immediately fallen in love with both of them. I had come to Fort Benning for the weekend, and we were all going to the Officers Club to celebrate my surviving my first year of teaching, plus there was a great band playing and Karen and Curt were fabulous dancers. After a delicious meal in the dining room, we went to the bar for champagne and dancing. It was very crowded, and I did notice Kincaid knew a lot of the people in the room. As the band started playing *Unchained Melody*, Kincaid said, "Elisabeth, we have to dance to your favorite song," and waltzed me out onto the dance floor.

Kincaid was being playful, dipping and twirling me—I assumed the champagne had gone to his head. As I spun around and stopped—the dance floor had cleared and there was Kincaid on his knee holding a beautiful diamond solitaire. "Elisabeth Belle Sterling, will you do me the honor of marrying me?" he asked.

Laughing and crying, I immediately answered, "Yes, Kincaid Patterson, I will marry you."

Then to the rousing cheer of fifty of Kincaid's Army buddies and friends, with the pull of a rope balloons and confetti fell from the ceiling, showering us all with happiness and me with a long kiss. "Why, Kincaid Patterson," I said, "underneath that stoic soul beats the heart of a true romantic."

"King Arthur at your service, M'lady," he said.

"Well, King Arthur, this was the most romantic proposal in all of Camelot."

"It is a good thing because you will not believe what the cleanup is costing me."

9

We set up our home in the tiny rented house Kincaid was living in several miles from base. I loved it. Of course, at that point, I would have been happy living in a tent in the middle of the Sahara Desert. Rather than confining, I found the smallness of the house quaint and cozy. All it needed was some feminine embellishments which I was glad to furnish. With my creative spirit and my limited sewing ability gleaned from Grandmother Reid, I turned the house on Magnolia Street into our home.

I got a job teaching second grade in an elementary school twenty minutes away. I soon found I loved teaching second graders. Seven-year-olds still thought their teacher was perfect, and they returned my love unabashedly. Added to this fact, the only subject I disliked more in school than math was chemistry, and in the second grade curriculum you did not even have to teach multiplication tables until the last six weeks of school. There were the usual stresses that went with any job, but I always had Kincaid to go home to and that tempered any stress a seven-year-old could throw at me.

As was bound to happen, slowly our differences began to emerge. I soon found it was hard to argue with Kincaid as he would just clam up. Since my passionate nature was prone to overreact, it worked and gave me time to come to my senses. But if a matter was important to me my stubbornness kicked in, and I insisted we talk it out. In a calm conversation, Kincaid was a great communicator. He just refused to shout. "What was the point of all my training arguing with Stewart if you refuse to yell?" I asked him.

I was inquisitive to a fault. I had not learned the art of talking with silence. When I would attempt to explain the unexplainable, he would say, "Eliza, sometimes there just are not words," and cover my mouth with long, lingering kisses. It had not taken Kincaid long to figure out that was a surefire way to shut me up.

My Southern penchant for apologizing, even when I was not at fault, was a constant irritant to Kincaid. One time when Kincaid was shopping with me, I had given the salesclerk a ten, a one, and four pennies for a $6.04 charge simply wanting a five dollar bill back. The poor girl was totally baffled, and I had apologized profusely for confusing her. "You know," Kincaid had said to me as we exited the store, "there was really no need to apologize. If a store hires someone to run a cash register, they really should be able to make change, don't you think."

"Hey, I'm not the one in the military where you are loath to admit mistakes," I reminded him.

"And that is a good thing. You would apologize to the enemy before you shot him."

Kincaid was the most rational and methodical person I had ever met, whereas my mind went careening off at the speed of lightning in a thousand different directions. One time, Kincaid was grocery shopping with me and as I was picking out rasp-berries, I said to him, "If I was on death row, I would request raspberries, fried chicken, and chocolate for my last meal."

Looking at me in total disbelief, Kincaid said, "You are the only person I know, not actually on death row, who knows what their last meal would be."

"Honestly, Kincaid, you have to be prepared in life."

Since the beginning of our relationship, I had cautiously broached the subject of his mother a couple of times but was firmly and emphatically rebuffed. Kincaid finally said, "Elisabeth, I thought I made it abundantly clear from the beginning my mother is no longer a part of my life, and I have no intention of discussing it. I am asking you to please respect that."

I am not a mysterious person but rather an open book, so of course, it worried me. When we had gotten engaged, I discussed it with my parents. My parents and Grandmother Reid had immediately loved Kincaid. They had sensed he was a good man, who would love and take care of their little girl. "Elisabeth," my very wise father had counseled, "I think there is something too painful for Kincaid to tell even you. Just give him time." So I bit my tongue, tamped down my impatient nature, and did not ask any more questions concerning his mysterious mother.

The biggest difference in our marriage was the matter of religion. It was actually more like a chasm. My belief in God had been heavily influenced by Grandmother Reid. She was one of the most serenely spiritual people I had ever encountered. As I spent time with my grandmother, her relationship with God was like osmosis as it gradually seeped into my being. Hers was not a God of solely Sunday morning worship but a vibrant, everyday God. Because of Grandmother Reid, my God became an invisible best friend, who was always there to hear my sorrows and my joys. Like my grandmother, God had been a vital part of my life as long as I could remember.

Because of the losses in Kincaid's relatively short life, he had a difficult time believing in a loving God. My relationship with God had brought such a peace to my life, even when my life was not peaceful; I wanted Kincaid to experience that too. It was a subject Kincaid would not discuss. I had started attending an Episcopal Church close to our home. It was a small congregation that welcomed newcomers in that warm way Southerners have. I immediately felt at home and loved Sunday mornings there. Kincaid flatly refused to entertain the idea of going with me. Kincaid was seldom stubborn except when it came to matters of religion and his mother.

The priest at the Episcopal Church was Father John, and we had immediately established a close rapport. I had gone to talk to him several times about Kincaid and his doubts concerning God. "Elisabeth," Father John had said, "you know change has to come from within a person. That is even truer for an unbeliever. Kincaid has to witness something he wants in his life, and he has to desire a deep longing for change. When these two experiences align is the greatest hope for an awakening. Unconditional love is the greatest gift someone can receive, which is a picture of God's love. Obviously, the only time in his youth Kincaid had experienced unconditional love was from his father, and in his mind, God abruptly took that from him when he needed it most. All you can do is love your husband unconditionally day in and day out. You, Elisabeth, are Kincaid's conduit to God's love." Father John paused. "I know I have only known you a short while, but I sense Kincaid and you have a very special marriage."

Suddenly from a depth unknown to me, tears starting flowing down my cheeks. Father John smiled his wise smile and patted me on the hand. "It's okay, Father John," I said, "these are tears of joy." So I took all the advice I had sought and loved my husband with the great capacity I had for love. Even as young and inexperienced as I was, I knew Kincaid and I had a very special relationship.

10

One afternoon in October, I got home from school and found the door to our house unlocked. Kincaid left after me in the morning, and he was usually so meticulous about locking the door. I cautiously stepped into the living room, but everything looked in place. Assuming Kincaid must have gotten a call from work and left in a hurry, I dropped my work satchel and went into our bedroom to change.

Startled, I put my hand to my mouth to stifle a scream because lying on our bed, sound asleep, was a strange person. Next to the bed sat a large, weathered bag, and my first thought was a homeless person had taken up residence in our house. My heart was racing as I tiptoed over to get a better look. It was a woman and something about her gnawed at the edges of my heart. I did not call the police. Instead, I called Kincaid. "Kincaid," I whispered urgently into the telephone when he answered, "did you leave the door unlocked today?"

"No, I always lock the door. I am very careful about that, and why are you whispering?"

"Well, you must have forgotten this morning because there is a homeless woman comfortably sleeping in our bed right this moment."

"What! Are you sure it is a homeless woman?" Kincaid asked.

"Well, it sure isn't Goldilocks, Kincaid."

I heard Kincaid take a quick gasp of breath as he said, "Stay right there, Elisabeth, I am coming straight home."

When Kincaid got home, he had a look on his face I had never seen, and when he came out of the bedroom, I sensed a lethal anger coiled tightly inside of him. He sat down and looked at me. "The woman asleep on our bed is my mother, Alysee Patterson."

To say I was stunned would be an understatement. "Your mother?"

"I am afraid so. Trust me, there is a story, and it won't be a pleasant one. Have you checked the liquor in the house because I have a suspicion she is not asleep but passed out?"

"Kincaid, I think all we have are a couple of beers in the refrigerator," I said as I went to look. "They are still there."

"Didn't Karen bring a bottle of tequila last week when they ate over here, so she could fix margaritas?"

"You're right, I forgot." I pulled the bottle from the cabinet. "Here it is. It is still almost full."

Kincaid handed me a glass. "Taste it," he said.

"Are you saying I need to get drunk before I meet your mother?"

"Just taste it."

I poured a small amount in the glass to taste. When the tasteless liquid hit my tongue, I said, "Oh my gosh, it's water!"

"Big surprise. It's the alcoholic's oldest trick. Now you see where I get my amazing wiles," Kincaid said with bitter sarcasm.

"Oh, Kincaid," I said touching him gently on the arm. "What are we going to do?"

"I will call Samson later tonight to find out the story. He won't be in from the boats yet. Trust me, Elisabeth, there is a reason Alysee has suddenly materialized, and it won't be a good one."

"Out of curiosity, how did Alysee get into the house if you locked the door? Do alcoholics have tricks for breaking into houses too?"

"Where do we leave our extra house key?"

"Under the flower pot by the front door."

"We leave our spare key in the same place, under the flower pot by the front door, that my father and I did when I was growing up. I guess some habits are ingrained for life."

"I am going to start cooking supper. Don't you imagine she'll get up in a few hours? Kincaid, I really do want to meet your mother."

Kincaid did not say anything. His jaw began to tense, and he was still coiled as tight as a rattlesnake ready to strike. I went into the kitchen to start dinner.

A few hours later, Alysee Patterson came into the kitchen, and I got my first good look at Kincaid's mysterious mother. She was thin and willowy, almost transparent. It seemed as if a gust of wind might snap her in two like an ice-laden twig on a bough, and the alcohol had taken its toll. Though only in her early forties, her skin was beginning to toughen and wrinkle, and her eyes were lusterless. Still, it was obvious she had at one time been a great beauty. She still retained a mass of black hair—that gorgeous mane she had bequeathed to Kincaid.

Kincaid was the first to speak. "Look, Elisabeth, it is my long-lost mother. I hear you've been playing Goldilocks, Mother. You gave Elisabeth quite a scare. So, what brings you to the Peach State?"

"You could at least say hello, Kincaid. I wanted to visit my son and his new wife. You didn't even bother to call and tell me you were married," Alysee answered.

"Well, Mother, you didn't even bother to raise me," Kincaid shot back.

Immediately I jumped in. "Please have a seat, Alysee. I am glad to meet you. I am working on my culinary skills, which are practically nonexistent. There is not a single culinary gene in any of my ancestors, so our best friend Karen is attempting to teach me to cook. So far, I have mastered spaghetti and meatballs and ravioli. Tonight is my inaugural attempt at manicotti. Suffice it to say, Karen is descended from a glorious line of raven-haired Italian cooks." I was babbling. Whenever there was tension, I suddenly metamorphosed into Pollyanna in an attempt to make the world right.

"Thank you, Elisabeth, I'm glad to meet you too. You're a very pretty girl, and that is a lot more important than being able to cook." Well, so much for being a deep person, I thought. Alysee continued, "I rode the bus all the way from Pascagoula. You meet some strange people on buses these days." I had to turn back to the stove to keep from laughing. "Manicotti sounds wonderful, Elisabeth, but I was wondering if I could have a little drink before we ate."

Kincaid got up. "Sure, Mother, we have some tequila in the cabinet. I'll get it for you."

Alysee turned pale. "Oh, Kincaid, do you have something else? I don't really drink tequila that much anymore."

"Sorry, Mother, that's all we have. You'll just have to suffer tonight," he said as he put a glass in front of her.

I am in the middle of a play, I thought, and I do not know whether it is a tragedy or a comedy. Somehow we made it through dinner and got Alysee back in bed as she really was at the point of exhaustion. Kincaid went to call Samson while I cleaned up. When Kincaid came back into the kitchen, there was sadness mixed with his anger. "As you can see, Elisabeth, Alysee is a desperate alcoholic. She was just picked up on her fourth DUI this year, and her last boyfriend deserted her. She was going to jail this time, so she ran away. Samson had a suspicion this was her destination."

"Kincaid," I said gently, "why don't you start at the beginning. I think it's time to tell me the whole story about your mother."

11

As I grew up and realized the extent of my mother's problems," Kincaid began, "my father started telling me about her background. A lot of it I found out from Samson after my father's death."

Alysee Broussard was born in the hardscrabble delta of Louisiana, the product of an abusive household. Her mother and father had both been physically beaten as children, and it was the only birthright they knew to pass on to their large brood of offspring. With thick black hair, dark eyes, and porcelain skin, Alysee Broussard was an exquisite beauty from the day she arrived on this earth. Her body developed with a sensuality that left men longing when she passed by.

Because of the turbulent circumstances of her upbringing, early in her life Alysee created a world that in her mind would allow her to escape the poverty and abuse that were her daily existence. As she matured, movies became her escape, and in her fragile mind Alysee became convinced she was headed toward stardom. For a few hours on Saturday afternoons, the dark movie theater in the small town became her salvation from the heavy fists of her father and the emotional abuse of her mother. After seeing *Casablanca* her first year in high school, Paris became her home and Humphrey Bogart her lover. She was Ingrid Bergman and Rita Hayworth all wrapped up in one package. Her senior year Alysee was crowned queen at the county fair, and this coronation gave her the motivation to strike out on her own.

"It was after her high school graduation that my mother managed to locate a distant cousin who lived in Pascagoula,"

Kincaid said. "She moved to Pascagoula that summer and started working in a local dress shop." Alysee's parents didn't seem to care; it was one less mouth to feed. Because of her striking looks and figure, Alysee was asked to do some modeling, and this with her recently acquired crown, cemented her belief that she was destined for Hollywood greatness.

Barrett Patterson had been running his father's shrimp boat for five years the summer he met the vivacious and striking Alysee. He fell in love with her beauty and her voracious appetite for life. The aura of otherworldliness that surrounded her made the nurturing Barrett want to enfold her in his arms and protect her. What Barrett failed to see was that the damaged Alysee was incapable of loving anyone, including herself. Forced to live in her own make-believe universe, Alysee had created a world of illusion that was not made to be shared.

Alysee was attracted to Barrett's quiet good looks, and they began dating. A year into their relationship Alysee got pregnant. Barrett was thrilled about the baby and immediately married her, but Alysee felt angry and trapped. Rather than softening these feelings intensified even more after Kincaid was born. Alysee's road to Hollywood did not include a husband and baby, and soon the realization sank in that this detour to stardom was permanent. Raised in a household with little love and compassion, Alysee had no role model for those emotions. To survive, she had embroidered her own elaborate imaginary world and ensconced herself into it like a butterfly in its cocoon, and nothing Barrett did could change that. This spun cocoon was Alysee's safety net, and she steadfastly clung to it. By the time Barrett came into Alysee's life, so much damage had been done that she was incapable of accepting her husband and son as a lifeboat, so she began to toss and thrash through life on a sure and steady collision course. Barrett and Kincaid could have been Alysee's redemption if she had only been able to internalize their unconditional love.

Within a year after Kincaid was born, Alysee was frequenting honky-tonks, drinking too much, and ending up in strange men's beds. Barrett had an oversized heart with compassion in abundance, and he could not bring himself to abandon Alysee though she had abandoned him and their son. Every few weeks, she would sober up and try her hand at domestication, but her efforts were futile. It was obvious her heart and mind were in her embellished cocoon. Alysee had lost her soul. Kincaid was raised by his father with visions of a lithe, dark butterfly floating in and out of his childhood, and the only bond Kincaid established was the paternal one.

"I might have been able to forgive my mother in some way if she had been there for me when my father died," Kincaid said with pain in his voice. "It's true, I was mature for my age, but, Elisabeth, I was only fifteen years old. I was devastated by my father's death." Rather than becoming the mother Kincaid so desperately needed, Alysee did the opposite. She drank more, stayed gone longer, and left Kincaid to raise himself. They lived off Social Security and his father's life insurance. The life insurance was set up in a trust fund with Samson as the trustee, so Alysee could not fritter it away. It was at this point Samson, Robbie Williams' parents, and his steadfast vision of West Point saved Kincaid's life.

As Kincaid finished talking, the sheer pain and torture of being abandoned by a mother were written all over the lines of his face. The pieces of the puzzle of Kincaid's mother had finally been joined together, and for one of the few times in my life, I was without words. I understood now why Kincaid had such a difficult time with the concept of a God who loves unconditionally. I knew how much I loved Kincaid before, but it was nothing compared to the depth of love I felt for him now. "Kincaid," I said softly as I took his hand, "you could have told me about your mother. I would have understood."

"Elisabeth, don't you see. I never had a mother. She was just a phantom drifting through my youth. Even now Alysee is true to form. She didn't come to see me or to meet my new wife. She was running away. Once I left Pascagoula for West Point, I never looked back. I have not been back to Pascagoula since. There is just too much pain. When I got to Fort Benning, I actually went to see a psychologist. I tried several appointments, but Elisabeth, I couldn't even talk to the psychologist about my mother. When I tried, I would get physically ill." Putting his other hand on top of mine, Kincaid looked at me and said, "The first time I felt emotionally alive since my father died was the minute I met you. You have been everything I could have hoped and more. You have saved my life, Elisabeth." I lost count of the number of times I had thanked God for putting Kincaid Patterson in my path, but I thanked him twice as much at that moment.

"What are we going to do, Kincaid?"

"If you can take a couple of days off, we will leave in the morning and take Alysee back to Pascagoula. Samson is arranging for Alysee's arraignment on Wednesday. She's going to jail this time. This is my mother's only hope to turn her life around."

The next morning while Kincaid and I were having coffee, Alysee walked into the kitchen. "Good morning, Alysee," I said, "how did you sleep?"

"I slept like the dead," she replied. "I was more tired than I realized. That bus ride wore me out."

"Would you like some coffee?"

"I would love some coffee, thank you. Well, Kincaid, aren't you going to speak? It's not every morning your mother is sitting in your kitchen having coffee with you."

"I talked to Samson. I know why you're here." I could hear the tension in Kincaid's voice. Alysee did not say anything. She slowly stirred her coffee and gingerly took a sip. "Elisabeth and I are taking you back to Pascagoula today. We're leaving in an hour. Your arraignment is tomorrow."

Alysee's hand started to shake and her face became pale. "Kincaid, you wouldn't do that, would you?" You could hear her voice on the precipice of panic. "If you would give me a little money, I could leave on the bus today. You could tell Samson I snuck out during the night."

"Mother," Kincaid said firmly, "it's over. This dream of yours that you call a life has come to an end. You no longer have a choice. All your bad choices have led to this."

"Kincaid, if you take me back, they will put me in jail. Do you want to put your mother in jail?"

"Mother, I did not put you in jail. You did that to yourself. If memory serves me correctly, I have not been a part of your life since you gave birth to me." Alysee flinched. "We are leaving in an hour," Kincaid said as he got up and left the room. I quickly followed. I was not going to give Alysee a chance to try and use me as an intermediary.

12

To Alysee's credit, once she saw the game was over, she sat silently in the back of the car. It was obvious she was not happy about any of it, but she held her tongue. Barely stopping along the way, we pulled into Pascagoula right at five hours. We stayed at Kincaid's childhood home, which Samson had been able to save by managing the trust fund. I could not imagine how hard this was on Kincaid or what was going through his mind, but he dealt with it all in his usual calm manner.

The next morning Samson met us at the courthouse. During the arraignment, Alysee stood straight as an arrow, totally without emotion. Underneath all the hurt and despair the remnants of a beautiful woman still lingered. The judge sentenced her to a year in the county jail. As the bailiff led Alysee away, she never turned to acknowledge any of us, not even her son. Alysee was once again wrapped in her own cocoon.

It was a delight to finally meet Samson. He had not been able to make it to our wedding because his wife, Thelma, had been ill. He was a huge bear of a man. "Your mother must have been omniscient when she named you," I said to him. "How did she know you would be like the Biblical Samson?"

"Elisabeth, you are just as pretty and sweet as Kincaid's been telling me. It's a relief to know I can quit worrying about this boy now that he has you to take care of him. Thelma sent some homemade biscuits for ya'll. Kincaid use to eat half a dozen every time he came to the house." It was all I could do to keep the tears at bay as we hugged Samson good-bye. Finally meeting the people who had meant so much to Kincaid was overwhelming.

On the way out of town, we stopped by to see Eleanor and Robert Williams, Robbie's parents. Robbie was living in Atlanta now and doing quite well in real estate, and he and his girlfriend had come to our wedding. Mr. and Mrs. Williams were thrilled to see Kincaid and could not have been any more gracious to me. We talked for a while about West Point, Fort Benning, and Kincaid's work. Mrs. Williams asked about my parents and my teaching. Kincaid wanted to apologize to the Williams for not keeping in touch but was having trouble finding the words. "Mr. and Mrs. Williams," he started, "I really feel bad about not keeping in touch. You meant so much..." Then Kincaid's voice broke.

Mrs. Williams immediately stepped in. "Kincaid," she said, "life has treated you unfairly, but you never whined or complained and always held your head high. Mr. Williams and I loved having you at our home. You were focused to a fault, and you know as well as I do, Robbie loved to have a good time. The way we see it you helped keep Robbie out of trouble until he could get some sense into him. We understand perfectly well why you never came back to Pascagoula, and we don't blame you a bit. That is all I am going to say about it, and I trust that puts the matter to rest. We will always love you like a son." There were tears all around as we said our good-byes. We got in the car to return to Columbus, and I knew what peace Mrs. Williams' words had brought to Kincaid.

As we traveled over the asphalt road and the miles clicked away, the sun began to set, and the horizon lit up with a splendid array of fiery reds and burnt oranges. The brilliant sunset gave way to a glorious night. Moment by moment, stars began to twinkle like bright-eyed tots on Christmas morning and then a full moon surrounded by a golden halo appeared. In my mind, it was God's way of telling Kincaid he had done the best he could with Alysee. As the night deepened, I felt the tension in Kincaid slowly begin to dissipate. Sliding over next to him, I gingerly laid my head on his broad shoulders. There was no need to say anything. That was one of the things I loved most about Kincaid. We could talk without words.

13

Curt Phillips and Kincaid had gotten to Fort Benning at the same time and hit it off immediately, and Karen, his wife, had "adopted" Kincaid. She and I had gotten to be very close in a short amount of time. Karen was shorter than I at five feet and was a little on the round side. She had flawless olive skin I envied and a head full of wavy black hair, courtesy of her Italian heritage. She had never met a stranger and was as down-to-earth as they come with loyalty that was boundless. I have always loved down-to-earth people. I have never been able to abide those disingenuous souls when the entire time they are talking you are thinking *what are they really saying*. You always knew where you stood with Karen.

Curt was 6 feet 4 inches and a solid 220 pounds. He had been a linebacker at Michigan State, where he met Karen, and he reminded me of a baby grizzly bear. As he was funny, kind, and loquacious, I had grown to love Curt dearly. From all appearances, Karen and Curt adored each other. Their two-year-old son, Colin, was a miniature of his mother but already sported the shape of his father. He was one of the happiest, most adorable toddlers I had ever seen. Karen was a wonderful mother. She was very hands-on and affectionate, but befitting her personality firm and strict when needed. Colin already knew he better not think about talking back to his parents and whining was out of the question. I had no doubt Colin would grow up to be a fine young man. You could just sense it.

When Karen walked in Saturday morning, I immediately knew something was not right.

I handed Karen a cup of coffee and said, "Talk."

"I'm not enjoying sex anymore." Karen was always one to get right to the point.

"Whoa," I said, "how long have you been married now?"

"Five years."

"Maybe it is just a temporary phase your body is going through," I said hopefully.

"I don't know, Elisabeth, I'm getting a little worried."

"Have you tried discussing this with Curt?" I asked.

"No, I'm not sure how to tactfully approach it," she said. "Quite frankly, I'm not exactly sure what's wrong. I can't put my finger on it. You know I adore Curt. He's the most wonderful husband and father in the world, so it's not that. Our sex life has always been very passionate, but for a while now it has been—I don't know—too routine." She took a sip of coffee. "I know you haven't been married quite a year, but it's obvious to everyone Kincaid and you have a very special relationship."

After Alysee's sudden visit last fall, I had told Karen the whole sad story about Kincaid's mother. "Kincaid may look like his mother," I said, "but that's where the similarity ends. He is decent to the core like his father. In psychobabble terms, I think our relationship is so good because Kincaid is thankful to have a woman who adores him who isn't incarcerated."

That night I told Kincaid about my conversation with Karen. "Really," he said looking genuinely surprised, "I would bet a lot of money Curt hasn't lost interest in sex."

"You know Curt better than anyone. Is there any chance there is someone else involved?" I asked.

"Absolutely no chance. The man worships the ground Karen walks on."

"Well, in that case, Kincaid," I said, "I have a plan." Kincaid groaned. My plans always struck fear in Kincaid's heart.

"I realize I am a sexual novice here, not ever having done the 'dirty deed' with anyone but you, but I have a theory. I think you should tactfully talk to Curt."

Totally unamused, Kincaid said, "Elisabeth, I am not talking to Curt Phillips about his sex life. I mean it. This discussion is over."

"You're going to make me take drastic measures," I threatened. He stood up, shook his head, and walked out of the room. He meant it. This discussion was over.

The next Saturday when I knew Karen had taken Colin to the park and Curt would be mowing the lawn, I went over to their house with lemonade for Curt. I was under no illusions that this would be easy. As far as I could remember, my parents had never uttered the word *sex* in my presence. I was pretty sure Stewart and I had been immaculately conceived. Mary Kate and I got all our sex education from any sex manual we could stealthily procure. I remember when I was in the eleventh grade, and a popular senior boy asked me out. We went to see Debbie Reynolds and Tony Curtis in the comedy *Goodbye, Charlie*. When Debbie Reynolds uttered the word "jock-strap" in the movie, I felt my face turn from shades of pink to crimson red, and I wanted to crawl under the nearest theater seat. I was actually relieved this boy, as popular as he was, never asked me out again. There was no doubt this was going to be a real challenge. But I plowed ahead, convinced my theory was correct.

After drinking the lemonade, Curt looked at me and said, "Okay, Elisabeth, what is it? You are acting like a cat on a hot tin roof."

"Curt, don't tell me you have read Tennessee Williams. You mean there is actually a brain in that big head?" I joked as he lobbed a wet cloth at me. "Okay, there's no easy way to do this, so I am going to get straight to the point. You need a little assistance with your sex life, and I am here to assist." Curt was speechless with his mouth agape. "Look, Curt, you can't take this personally. Let's just say I am going on a hunch. I think it's a mechanics issue, and I have a plan," I said triumphantly.

By this point, Curt was practically sputtering. "I can't believe I am hearing this."

"I know, it's amazing. I am not exactly a sex siren. But admit it, Curt, things have been a little cool lately in the bedroom, haven't they?" I had his attention even though I could tell he was none too happy about the direction of this conversation. "Just do me a favor and try one thing. If it doesn't work, I promise to never butt into your sex life again."

All Curt could do was shake his head and say, "This is truly unbelievable," but I could tell he was intrigued.

"Next time Karen and you have sex I want you to do everything but…" I hesitated here. I truly did not know if I could actually say it. "Everything but…"

I saw a slight smile come on Curt's face at my discomfort. "Everything but what, Elisabeth?" He was clearly enjoying the tables turned.

"Everything but sexual intercourse," I said as fast as I could, sliding over the "sexual intercourse" part.

Curt looked at me like I had gone slap-dab crazy. "You want me to have sex without having sex? Wow, Elisabeth, what a great idea! Can I go find Karen and get started on this novel plan right away? I can hardly wait. The excitement is killing me."

"Honestly, Curt, you can be such a smart ass."

"And you need to give up your job as a sex therapist and go back to teaching."

I ignored him because, quite frankly, I was a woman on a mission. "Look, do everything else, just don't actually have sex for the next few times even if Karen begs you. I mean she probably won't beg you at first. It may take a few times. Curt, if you aren't having actual sex, you'll have to get creative probably like you did in the beginning of your sex life. You're a smart man. I have complete confidence you can figure it out. I don't have to draw you a blueprint."

"You're serious, aren't you?"

"Dead serious." Curt was actually a very intelligent man and deep down quite sensitive. I really thought I was getting through.

"What if she never begs me?"

"Well, Curt, then you have a bigger problem than I think, and you will probably have to invest in a real sex therapist. But right now I'm all you've got," I said giving him my most saccharine smile.

"You are truly insane, Elisabeth."

"For Pete's sake, quit all the bellyaching. This advice is not costing you a penny." Curt growled and grumbled like the ersatz grizzly bear he was, but I could tell I had piqued his interest.

The next few weeks were extremely busy at school. Spring had sprung, and my creative juices had kicked up a notch. When that happened, I became a whirling dervish. Kincaid had been known to lock himself into the bathroom just to get some peace and quiet. Plus, it was the only place to sit as my latest project was a musical rendition of *The Three Little Pigs*, and every surface in our tiny house was covered with tempera paint, papier-mâché, and glitter.

"Why are you doing a musical?" Kincaid asked in exasperation one day. "You do know you sing like a frog."

"What is it with you dumb boys? Adam Presley told me the same thing when I was twelve. By now, I am quite aware of the fact I sing like a frog. It is very rude to say that to anyone, much less to the person you supposedly love more than anything in the world. Besides, I have a parent who is teaching all the musical parts."

The musical version of *The Three Little Pigs* was a smashing success. One of the best things about seven-year-olds is the more mistakes they make the more endearing they are. It had been three weeks since we had seen Karen and Curt, so we made plans to go to our favorite Mexican restaurant followed by drinks and dancing at a nearby night club. We had a special reason to celebrate as Kincaid had been promoted to First Lieutenant. For the occasion, I wore my blouse with the off-the-shoulder, brightly colored ruffles that I had purchased for school when we had studied Mexico.

At the first slow dance, Kincaid asked Karen to dance and Curt grabbed me. "I put Kincaid up to that because I wanted to talk to you," Curt said. "It worked." For a moment, I was puzzled, and then I remembered and gave him my huge I-told-you-so smile. "I loved the begging so much I almost didn't give in," Curt said with a boyish grin.

"Why, Curt Phillips, you big oaf, you are such a martyr."

"Yeah, I decided I could be a martyr," he teasingly said.

"What life lesson have we learned from this little experiment?" I asked.

"It is better to give than receive?" he asked with a gleam in his eye.

"How about 'the joy you give to others is the joy that comes back to you,'" I said laughingly.

Curt swirled me around the dance floor and said, "Elisabeth Belle, you very wise woman, I owe you big time for this one. You are a jewel."

"You won't think that when you get my bill."

Laughing, we waltzed back to the table to give a toast to best friends and my dazzling success as a sex therapist.

14

It was hard to believe, but August was fast approaching, bringing with it our first wedding anniversary and my twenty-fourth birthday. The year had flown by, yet I felt like Kincaid and I had been together for years. He was becoming so much a part of me that I could not imagine my life without him. My normally stoic husband was actually getting excited about these intertwining events. He refused to let me plan one solitary thing for the day. To my recollection, it was the first day of my life I started without making a plan. "But how will I know what to wear?" I complained. "Unlike a man, for a woman these earthshaking decisions cannot be left to chance."

"A swimsuit and a sexy dinner dress will do it. After that, clothes will not be necessary," he said with a leer.

We slept in on the big day and around ten o'clock the doorbell rang. Opening the door, I was presented with a long-haired teenage boy holding one long-stemmed red rose. "Are you Elisabeth Belle Patterson?" he asked.

"Yes," I said slowly.

"This is for you."

"Well, Roy," I said spying his name on the florist jacket, "you must have the wrong Elisabeth Belle Patterson because I only see one rose in that vase you're holding."

Roy looked at the card and said, "Is this 712 Magnolia Street?"

"Yes, it is."

"Then this is the right place."

"Roy, do you think in your haste you might have left some roses in the van?"

"No, ma'am, I'm sure this is what was ordered."

"Is there by any chance a rose shortage this year?"

Poor Roy stared at me, clutching the single rose, unsure of what to do next. Kincaid came to his rescue, took the rose, tipped him, and said, "Thank you, Roy. My wife forgot to take her meds this morning," as he closed the door.

"Happy Anniversary, Eliza," Kincaid said as he handed me the rose.

"I am sure there is a logical explanation for this lonely flower."

"How many years have we been married?" Kincaid asked.

"One."

"How many roses do you see in the vase?"

"One."

"Okay, Elisabeth, this is the way I see it. If I get you a dozen roses every year for fifty years, you would get a total of 600 roses. On the other hand, if on our anniversary I buy you a rose for each year we have been married in fifty years you will have gotten 1275 roses." Kincaid was annoyingly good at math.

"Let me get this straight. If I live with you for fifty years, I get 1275 roses?"

"Bribery has never been beneath me," Kincaid said with a lopsided grin.

Finally, I smiled and said, "Wow, Kincaid, who knew beneath that macho facade of yours beats the heart of a romantic! You do realize there's not a snowball's chance in hell you'll get me to leave now."

As Kincaid gathered me in his arms and carried me to our bedroom, he said, "That, Madam, is my foolproof plan. I have yet to meet a woman who can turn down roses."

An hour later I murmured, "That solitary rose is growing on me, Kincaid. It is definitely growing on me."

We spent the afternoon at a crystal-blue lake where we swam, ate lunch, and talked about how lucky we felt to have found each other. Kincaid had packed raspberries, fried chicken, and chocolate truffles in the picnic basket. "This is just in case you never make it to death row," he laughed as he tousled my wet hair.

For that evening, Kincaid had made dinner reservations at one of the nicer dining establishments in Columbus. About 6:20, Kincaid strolled into our bedroom. My feet were propped on a pillow while I was waiting for my toenail polish to dry. Kincaid was acting strange, walking around very anticipatory like. "What is wrong with you? You're acting like Stewart the time he put a frog in my bed."

Kincaid's eyes kept going to the clock by my bed. Finally he said, "Elisabeth, what time of the day were you born?"

"I haven't the slightest idea."

"I'll give you a clue. Look at the clock."

Looking at the clock, it said 6:22. When I turned my head back around, there was my husband, with a goofy smile on his face, holding a gift beautifully wrapped in shiny gold paper with the largest white satin bow on top I had ever seen.

"Let me guess. I was born at 6:22 P.M."

"Happy Birthday, Eliza."

I jumped up and gave Kincaid the biggest hug I could manage. "How did you know the time of my amazing birth?"

"I went straight to the source—your mother."

"I guess she would know that. But, Kincaid, I am a little scared to open this gorgeously wrapped present. After the roses, it might be one stone of a bracelet where I have to wait fifty years to complete it," I teased him.

"I cajoled the salesgirl into making an extra big bow," he said, obviously very pleased with his efforts.

It was indeed a splendidly wrapped gift. With my usual impulsiveness, I tore the paper off in record time. There nestled in a velvet box lay an exquisite emerald and pearl necklace. I let out a shriek and covered Kincaid with kisses. "Emerald and pearls—my two favorites. My mother?"

"Your mother is a wealth of information." Kincaid gingerly clasped the delicate necklace around my throat. As he gently kissed the hollow of my neck, he whispered, "Dinner reservations aren't until eight."

"Whatever will we do until then?" I asked.

"I have an outstanding idea," he replied.

"I don't suppose you purposely made dinner reservations late?"

"Whatever would give you such an idea?" my husband asked as he gently pushed me onto the bed.

At dinner that night over filet mignon, lobster, and champagne, I gave him my present. It was a lovely leather kaleidoscope mother had helped me find in an antique shop in Atlanta on one of our shopping excursions. "This reminds me of you, Elisabeth Belle. The colors are bright and interesting and running off in all directions."

We toasted our good fortune. We toasted Jane for insisting I go on the blind date. I even toasted my emerald and pearl necklace. "Kincaid, I must say, I had my doubts when Roy made his delivery this morning, but you have outdone yourself. That one rose is looking better and better. The way I see it, I don't really have a choice. What girl can turn down over one thousand roses even if it does take fifty years?"

One of my favorite stories of Grandmother Reid's was what she called her "Red Letter Day." On a trip to Savannah, my grandfather had bought her a diamond ring and a mink stole on the same day. That night as I snuggled in Kincaid's arms, I whispered, "Grandmother Reid, I just had my Red Letter Day."

15

Kincaid and I spent Thanksgiving in Hillston. Coming home from school the next week, I made a serious mistake. I thought to myself that life was too good to be true. Driving up to our house, I was surprised to see Kincaid's Fairlane in the carport. It was very rare for him to come home in the afternoon and I hoped he was not sick, but then Kincaid never got sick.

When I walked into the house, Kincaid was sitting on the sofa, and I knew from the look on his face something serious had happened. I sat down next to him without saying a word. I do not deal with adversity well, so my plan was to delay any bad news as long as I could. Finally, Kincaid took my hands, looked me in the eyes, and said, "Elisabeth, I'm being deployed to Vietnam."

I was absolutely stunned. I felt like someone had hit me in the stomach, and I literally could not breathe. Then I lost it and fell completely apart. First, I started screaming, "No, they can't do this. The war in Vietnam is winding down, not escalating. They are bringing soldiers home. Nixon himself said the 'end is in sight.' No, no, no!" The frustration and fear were so intense I began throwing pillows and magazines—I threw a pair of shoes—anything within close range. This sophomoric reaction surprised even myself. Kincaid just sat on the sofa patiently watching me. Then when my furor was spent, he gently gathered me in his arms and let me sob until there were no more tears.

The fear of deployment to Vietnam had, of course, always been there. No matter how you tried, you could not escape it. There was a constant barrage of war news on the television and in the papers. College campuses were erupting with anti-war sentiment. It was true, in the past year, record numbers of soldiers had departed Vietnam. But, all that aside, America was fighting a very real war, and soldiers were dying. In my usual ostrich stance, I had pushed this fear down as far as it would go and stuck my head in the sand. In my way of thinking, America had been fighting in Vietnam for almost seven years now, and the Army was bringing soldiers home. Surely that meant a peace treaty was on the horizon. But as Kincaid explained, a yearlong tour of duty was the norm, and America was still fighting—so soldiers were still being sent to Vietnam. He was in military intelligence and needed. We always knew deployment was a possibility, but I had just refused to even remotely acknowledge it.

Kincaid was due to leave the beginning of January, and it was one of the saddest Christmases I had ever spent. I was acting so childish my mother actually berated me. "Elisabeth Belle, you have to grow up. You are not the first wife whose husband has gone to war. Think about Kincaid. You are making it harder on him." As usual, my mother was right, and I was justly shamed. I tried to get it together after my mother's admonishment.

Our last night before Kincaid left was intensely sad, but intensely beautiful. We made love like a movie in slow motion. Knowing the memory would have to last us for the next year, we relished every gesture, savored every touch. For months afterward, I replayed this last night over and over in my mind. Some days it was the only thing that kept me sane.

Kincaid's plane was leaving early in the morning, and the time came for him to go. When he walked back in the bedroom dressed, I was sitting cross-legged in the middle of the bed, my hair a tangled mess, tears furiously streaming down my face. He took me in his arms and kissed me gently, passionately, because there were no more words and walked out the door. I had told

Kincaid I could not watch him leave—it would be too painful—and he had understood. I do not know how long I sat there because time ceased, but the sudden realization came to me that for the next year this is the way Kincaid would remember his wife—sitting in the middle of the bed, a sobbing mess.

Fast as lightning, I washed my face, brushed my hair, and dressed. Rushing out of the house, I got to the airfield as the soldiers were walking to the plane. As though he sensed something, Kincaid turned and saw me standing there. He put his hand over his heart, and his face lit up with his beautiful smile as he boarded the plane. Kincaid's last sight before boarding was of me standing behind the gate with my blonde hair blowing in the wind and a smile on my face. I looked like a very brave woman sending her husband off to war when, in fact, there was nothing brave about me at all. I turned, suddenly blinded by my tears, and there were Karen and Curt. We encircled each other and cried like we had lost our best friend because, in fact, we had.

16

Dear Kincaid,
Everyone says I should write positive thoughts so you won't get depressed, but it ain't gonna happen. You wouldn't believe me anyway. You know better than anyone that I am an open book.

I miss you so much it hurts physically and emotionally. In case you haven't picked up on it in the last year and a half, I REALLY love sex (note the capital letters). You are an amazing teacher, and I cannot wait until you are holding me in your arms again. I REALLY miss having conversations with you (note the capital letters). I do realize I do most of the talking. Like my mother says, "Is there any thought that does not come out of your mouth?" But when you do talk, you are very wise or very funny. It is no fun laughing at my own jokes, which is a lie as I have not laughed since you left. Also I REALLY hate taking out the garbage (note the capital letters). It stinks, and I wait so long it gets very heavy.

I also told you, early in our relationship, I dislike martyrs, so it should come as no surprise to you I am a terrible one. I have pretty much whined since you left. My parents have quit taking my calls. Not really, I am their child, so they have to listen to me.

I would write some news, but there isn't any. Oh yeah, America is fighting a war in Vietnam, of all places. Seven years ago, eighty percent of Americans could not even find Vietnam on a map. Now we are shooting at each other. So much for my stab at humor, but I will write news when I get out of my depression and actually leave the house.

Karen misses you terribly too, but I have no sympathy for her as she is still having sex—wonderful sex, somewhat thanks to me and my dazzling, albeit short-lived, career as a sex therapist. Even Curt is moping around. There is no one to laugh at his corny jokes as Karen and I refuse to lower ourselves to his level of humor. When I stopped by the other day, Colin kept asking for "K," so of course, I started bawling and had to leave.

Well, that is all the uplifting news I have for now. I am going out this afternoon to spend all our savings on a new emerald and pearl ring to match my incredibly gorgeous anniversary necklace. That should cheer me up.

On a serious note, our last night together was one of the most beautiful nights of my life even with the sadness. I have never felt closer or more a part of you. In your very wise way, your last words to me were uniquely Kincaid—"Save my place."

Your place is saved and I love you deeply,

Eliza

P.S. I am not really going to go out and blow our savings on an emerald and pearl ring.

17

Dear Kincaid,
Good morning! Settle in and get ready for an enticing read since I doubt *Days of Our Lives* is broadcast on the Mekong Delta. Thanks to my dear and dramatic friend Mary Kate, I was recently involved in my own personal soap opera. You know there is nothing like a soap opera to perk me up as I am such a sucker for high drama. Mary Kate, who you recall still lives in Atlanta, called me with the disturbing news she was fairly certain that her husband Bruce was having an affair. I will have to admit Mary Kate does have a keen sense about people, which makes it even more of a mystery why she chose to marry Bruce Davidson. She recently had to go to a teacher's conference in Athens for a Saturday, and Bruce told her he was going to a man's get-away at the lake house of a college friend. Being suspicious, Mary Kate got this college friend's phone number and called that Saturday on some fabricated pretense. The friend answered, and Mary Kate ascertained enough to know he was spending the Saturday at home with his wife and child. It was obvious he knew nothing about Bruce's conjured plans at his lake house.

At this point, Mary Kate's latent actress genes ratcheted up a notch. If I am the Sandra Dee of Hollywood, then Mary Kate is Katharine Hepburn. In all her finest glory, she came up with a most elaborate entrapment plan. If you need help capturing the

Viet Cong, Mary Kate is your gal. She told Bruce she was going to Columbus to spend the weekend with me as I was in a serious state of the doldrums. That part, Kincaid, is true. Life without you is seriously awful, not to digress from my soap opera. True to form, Bruce told her he was going hunting with another college buddy. He apparently has no shortage of fictional college friends. She took that Friday off from work, and as soon as Bruce came home to get his bags, Mary Kate left for her weekend with me. This is where it really gets interesting, Kincaid. Meanwhile, I had rented a car so we would be incognito, driven to Atlanta, and was lurking around the corner of their house. Mary Kate jumped in my rental car, and as soon as Bruce screeched out of their driveway, we discreetly followed him.

About an hour out of Atlanta, Bruce exited and drove to a Holiday Inn. "At least it isn't the Hyatt Regency," Mary Kate quipped. This part, Kincaid, will make you upset with me as you have this strange idea I should stay out other people's sex lives. But honestly, Kincaid, the drama was just too good to pass up. After Bruce went inside the Holiday Inn, I stealthily entered the lobby and furtively hide behind the largest palm tree I could locate. It felt like I was in a 'fifties movie. Bruce was at the registration desk when, sure enough, up walked a bleached blonde with big hair, big boobs, and the shortest miniskirt allowed by law. Miss Big Hair lovingly whispered some sweet nothing in his ear, he laughed, and they turned to walk to the elevator. As Bruce much too casually draped his arm around Miss Miniskirt's shoulders, and she hooked her apple-red polished claws around his waist, I sauntered out from behind the shelter of the palm tree.

"Why, Bruce Davidson," I said in my best mocking tone, "imagine meeting you at an out-of-the-way Holiday Inn and with a blonde strapped to your arm." Kincaid, I wish you could have seen Bruce's face. At first, he was totally transfixed, but as realization set in, his face blanched as white as a baby's butt. It still had not sunk in Miss Big Boob's small amount of brain cells that this encounter might very well put a damper on her little tryst. Since I do not know CPR and it appeared Bruce was going to have a heart attack, I chose that moment to make my Oscar-winning exit. "I'll tell your WIFE, Mary Kate, you send your regards from—where is it—a hunting lodge." And, with a flounce of my head, I sashayed out of the gold and green lobby of the Holiday Inn. I figured that was enough histrionics for one day.

Not to make light of a very sad situation, Mary Kate was quite shaken up. Deep down she knew the truth, but it has to be intensely painful to admit to yourself you have married a complete cad. Bewildering as it is to me, it turns out she really loves Bruce. I drove Mary Kate back to Columbus where she got as inebriated as I have ever seen her. The entire next day, I fed her aspirin and held her head as she wailed about her stupidity for falling in love with a rogue such as Bruce Davidson. "I want you to know, Elisabeth," she sobbed, "I am really good in bed. I adore sex. I honestly thought Bruce was happy."

"Mary Kate," I assured her, "you know as well as I do this has nothing to do with you or sex. This is a deep fault line in Bruce's character. The last thing you are going to do is take the blame for any of this." As I write, Bruce is in a state of contrition, but Mary Kate has wisely kicked him out for the time being. Not to take divorce lightly, but I personally think she needs to wash her hands of his sorry butt, close this chapter in her life, and chalk it up to life experience. Only time will tell what Mary Kate decides, but you will be proud of me as I am keeping my mouth shut. I do realize this is a decision that Mary Kate needs to make totally on her own.

Sunday on the drive back to Atlanta, Mary Kate wanted me to describe in detail the whole dramatic episode. I actually had her in tears with laughter, and she presented me an Academy Award. Like Mary Kate said, "You just have to laugh at life or you would surely go crazy." I am going to have to admit to you, Kincaid, that it is a real challenge finding some humor in your being ten thousand miles away where people are shooting at you. During this whole distasteful incident with Bruce, I kept thinking Kincaid would never have an affair. I sense it to the very core of my being. So I will close our little soap opera for now.

Thank you, Kincaid, for being the type of man I trust explicitly even on the other side of the world. Your place is saved.

I love you deeply,
Eliza

P.S. Where do you think I should display my Oscar?

18

February 27, 1972
Sunday afternoon

Dear Kincaid,
How are you? I trust fine and taking care of yourself. I have two big pieces of news. First, I am a star! I decided I had moped around enough and needed to do something creative. You know how hyper I get when I embark on one of my "projects." So I gave each of my second graders a square of white cloth and asked them to draw a picture with permanent magic markers signing their name to their drawing. I went to Hillston for the weekend where Grandmother Reid and my mother helped me sew all the squares together and then make a dress for myself. You should have seen the faces of those seven-year-olds when I walked into the classroom Monday morning. My principal was so impressed she called the local newspaper, and there I was the following Friday on the front page of the local section with my twenty-four cherubs broadly smiling at me. I have a cramp in my hand from signing all those autographs!

Next, in my ongoing quest for some semblance of culinary proficiency, I decided to tackle lasagna. Karen was scheduled to help me, but Colin developed an ear infection, and she had to take him to the pediatrician. Not to be deterred and armed with Karen's mother's recipe, which I am positive is one hundred years old, I set about assembling a worthy lasagna. Let me insert a note here that lasagna from scratch is not an easy task for the best of chefs, but with my limited culinary ability, it was downright daunting. Amazingly, all was going well. In fact, I was quite pleased with myself.

The recipe failed to mention the exact size of the lasagna pan, so I had just grabbed one I assumed would work. The size of the pan really did not seem that important in the overall scheme of lasagna-making. I did notice the pan seemed a bit full, but I just squished all those layers down and stuck it in the oven. Since lasagna has to bake for thirty minutes, I settled down to read. I am reading *The Godfather* as I want to read the book before I see the movie, plus it seemed appropriate since I was making lasagna. I was lost in the intrigues of the Corleone family when I suddenly smelled smoke. Rushing into the kitchen, I saw thick, black smoke and angry, yellow flames billowing from the oven. Instantly realizing that this was past baking soda, and probably even a fire extinguisher, I immediately called the fire department. They were there within ten minutes and had the fire out within twenty minutes. Needless to say, all that commotion caused quite a stir in the neighborhood. It seemed the lasagna had majorly boiled over and caught the oven on fire. As Karen later pointed out, my pan was half the size I needed. The firemen and neighbors could not have been nicer. One of the firemen mentioned I might want to try take-out the next time! Kincaid, you would have been so proud of me as I was calm and collected the entire time. For some reason, a little fire did not seem like the end of the world. The fact is your being gone is the end of the world.

Except for some smoke damage and a completely defunct oven, everything else was fine. I called our landlord and Mr. Henry was very kind. His insurance covered everything, which is a very good thing as our rental contract does not allow for burning down the house. Imagine that! So this week the cleaners came and took care of the smoke damage, and Mr. Henry had a new oven installed. It is a very nice oven—much superior to the one I destroyed, I might add. Karen is still in dismay that I used such a small pan for such a large amount of lasagna. I tried to explain to her that logic was never my forte.

Now to give you an update on Mary Kate. Mary Kate still has not let Bruce come back home. I say good riddance to him, but it is obvious she still loves the cad. So, as I have said before, only time will tell how that little soap opera plays out. I am trying to spend as much time with Mary Kate as I can.

If being without your husband was supposed to get any easier, I want to be the first to tell you it is not. I miss you more than ever with each day that passes. Thank you for your wonderful letter. I read it every night before I go to sleep. Your place is saved.

I love you deeply,
Eliza

P.S. I forgot to tell you. Robert Redford called yesterday and asked me to have dinner with him. Being the loyal wife I am, I declined. You owe me—big time.

19

March 11, 1972
Saturday night

Dear Kincaid,
Hello! Tonight I am going to regale you with the tales of a second grade school teacher as it has been quite an entertaining week. I know you remember me talking, or rather bellyaching, about Louis. He is big for a seven-year-old and always testing me to my limit. Louis struggles with learning and tries to make up for it by being a bully. He has a wonderful personality, but his low self-esteem keeps getting him into trouble. I have tried so hard to build him up in other ways—for example, he is very athletic. But the last straw came when he pushed poor little Andrew, who is sweet as pie and half his size. Coming from lunch, the class was walking in line in the hallway. Andrew was not paying attention when we stopped, and he accidentally ran into Louis. Louis, of course, overreacted and pushed Andrew so hard he knocked over Trisha. My last nerve snapped, and I grabbed Louis saying, "You are going to the principal's office, now!"

Well, Louis did not think that was such a grand idea. Right there in the middle of the hallway, he dug in his heels and started bellowing at the top of his lungs, "NO, I'M NOT GOING."

"Oh yes, you are," I answered as I grabbed both of his hands from the front and started trying to pull him down the hall to the office. The harder I pulled the more he dug in his heels and the louder he yelled. Bear in mind, Louis is almost my height and weight. I looked like a farmer trying to budge a braying mule. You can imagine the ruckus all this was causing.

Finally Mrs. Harvard, the third grade teacher, came out of her room. Mrs. Harvard is almost six feet tall and the size of a Georgia Tech linebacker. She flew over to Louis, picked him up by the seat of his pants, and said, "That's enough, young man. You're going to the principal's office like Mrs. Patterson said," and dragged him off. Mrs. Harvard really is a wonderful teacher, and once the children get in her classroom they end up loving her, but with her size and deep, gruff voice the little ones are scared to death of her. My remaining twenty-three pupils had pupils the size of saucers. Andrew and Trisha were fine, and Louis returned to the classroom thirty minutes later and genuinely apologized to me, Andrew, and Trisha. I honestly think he even surprised himself with that little outburst.

I profusely thanked Mrs. Harvard for saving the day and keeping me from looking like a complete fool. As I told her, "Mrs. Harvard, Louis was not budging, and I was at the end of my options."

She said, "Elisabeth, it was all I could do to keep a straight face. You were a sight to see trying to drag that child down the hallway. I have got size and a mouth over you."

The next day I learned that size was not the only thing some of my second graders had over me. It was Friday after lunch and I was teaching a reading group. It had been a long day, and the story about a visit to the zoo was going extraordinarily slow. Finally, I closed the book and said, "That's enough reading for today. Let's play charades and act out our favorite zoo animals." The kids were having a grand time guessing each other's animal when Lionel, who you will remember is the class clown, said, "Mrs. Patterson, you play."

"Okay, Lionel, I'll play."

So Lionel walked over to me and whispered in my ear, "You be a giraffe." Well, I was doing my very best giraffe imitation when Lionel jumped up and yelled, "I know, I know, you're a giraffe." So, Kincaid, there you have it—I was outsmarted by a seven-year-old.

To end the week on a high note, we always do art on Friday afternoon. David spilled red paint on my white blouse, so right then and there, I painted a clown with a big red nose on the front of my shirt. The kids were delighted. Let's just pray they do not decide to try it at home, or I will be the one going to the principal's office Monday morning. Kincaid, I can hear you laughing right now. Your eyes just got crinkly, and then you let out your wonderful laugh that comes from deep inside of you. It's not like my high hyena laughter but a rich, robust kind. I am counting the days until I hear that laughter again.

So that ends it for my week. I hope your week has been calm. I miss you terribly, Kincaid. I am finding laughter does help. Your place is saved.

I love you deeply,
Eliza

P.S. Please dodge all bullets. Maybe you could find someone the size of Curt or Samson and hide behind them. Just a suggestion.

20

Dear Kincaid,
I hope you are sitting down because I have pulled a tour de force. Seriously, you better sit down. First, I need to establish the cast of characters. I know you remember sweet Jenny in my class. Last summer, they discovered she had a malignant brain tumor. Her surgery was very successful, but the doctors had to follow up with aggressive chemotherapy. Jenny has responded beautifully to her treatments, and her prognosis is very good, but of course, she lost all her hair from the chemotherapy treatments and she still has a few treatments left. She started the school year wearing her wig, but she really hated wearing it as it was very uncomfortable. We had some class discussions, and soon Jenny was coming to school just wearing her cute hats. Everyone has been very accepting and kind to her.

Marvin entered my classroom a couple of weeks after you left for Vietnam. His parents seem very nice, but his family is large and they have moved around quite a bit. Marvin seems very unsettled, and I suspect he has a learning disability. He has had a very hard time making friends.

Last Monday the class had physical education at the end of the day, and I was on my way to get them. As I rounded the corner of the building, there was Marvin imitating a monkey while laughing at Jenny and telling her she looked like a monkey with her bald head. Her hat was on the ground, so I assumed Marvin had snatched it off of her head. Poor tiny Jenny was huddled against the brick building sobbing her little heart out, and my heart cracked in two. Kincaid, I have never been so infuriated in my entire life, and I was shaking all over I was so angry. I took Marvin by the shoulders, put him against the wall of the building, and told him he better not move until I got back. He had never seen me that angry or upset, so he knew he better not budge. Somehow I got Jenny to the health room and Marvin and the rest of the class dismissed. Jenny's mother picks her up everyday, so I talked to her mother and called Marvin's parents before he got home on the school bus.

Then I had an epiphany! Are you still sitting down, Kincaid? Before I lost my nerve, I drove straight to Vicki, who cuts my hair, and ask her to shave my head. Of course, she refused, but I told her the entire story. She did it against her will, but Kincaid, she shaved my head. That's right—I am now baldheaded! I mean it's not like I had hair like Rapunzel—it's no great loss—but I do look a bit different.

Kincaid, you should have seen my second graders the next morning when I walked into the classroom. Every single one of them looked like a deer caught in the headlights, and they were all slack-jawed. The first thing I noticed was that Jenny was wearing her wig. Finally Lisa said, "Mrs. Patterson, you shaved your head."

"Now that you mention it, Lisa, I did. Class, let me ask you a question. Am I still Mrs. Patterson?" Still in shock, some nodded, and I heard a few "Yeses." "So even without hair I am still your same teacher?" Again there were some nods and a few "Yeses." Then I wrote in large letters on the chalkboard "DOES IT MATTER?" Walking around the room, I said, "Trisha, does it matter if my eyes are blue?"

"No, ma'am," Trisha answered.

"Bert, does it matter if I have brown eyes?"

89

"No, ma'am," Bert said.

"Jason, does it matter if my skin is white?"

"No, ma'am."

"Louis, does it matter if I have brown skin?"

"No, ma'am."

"Nick, does it matter if I wear old jeans with beat-up tennis shoes?"

"No, ma'am," Nick replied.

"Elizabeth, does it matter if I wear a frilly lace dress with shiny patent leather shoes?"

"No, ma'am."

"Chip, does it matter if I have blonde hair?"

"No, ma'am."

"John, does it matter if I have no hair?"

"No, ma'am," John said.

Then I came to Marvin, who was looking down at his feet. "Marvin, look at me." He looked up. "Marvin, does it matter how I act?"

"Yes, ma'am," Marvin said in a whisper.

"Marvin, I think you have something to say to Jenny."

Marvin turned to Jenny and quietly said, "Jenny, I'm sorry I laughed at you. I think you're beautiful."

I turned Marvin to me and said, "Thank you, Marvin. You just did the right thing."

As I walked to the front of the room, I saw Jenny take off her wig and then she walked up to me, hugged her thin arms around my waist and buried her bald head in the folds of my dress. Kincaid, if I had any doubts about my rash action, they dissipated in that heartfelt moment.

Taking a lesson from my father, each Monday I put a new word on the board for the class to learn the definition and use in sentences throughout the week. I said, "Class, you can see I have added another word for this week. The word is empathy, and its definition is: being aware of and sharing another person's feelings, experiences, and emotions. You see, I have shared one of Jenny's experiences—by being bald, I now know how Jenny feels. Class, if you only learn one lesson this school year, learn to have empathy for other people."

Needless to say, Kincaid, I fielded phone calls all week. I guess it was a rather dramatic act. The teachers and parents were shocked I had actually done such a daring thing but were equally impressed, especially Jenny's parents. I got so tired of people staring at me when I went places other than school that my mother met me in Atlanta on Saturday and bought me a beautiful—sit down again, Kincaid—strawberry red wig. I have always wanted to be a redhead, so I figured now was my chance. I will probably wear it everywhere except home and school. Vicki assured me healthy hair grows half an inch a month, so by my calculations by the time you get home, I will have four to five inches of hair—short, but not bald.

Thus ends my theatrics, Kincaid—you can stand up now. I am more than sad you are not here to share in the thrilling life of a school teacher. What little we make in pay is made up in adventure. I do miss you terribly—it makes me do crazy things. Your place is saved.

I love you deeply,
Eliza

P.S. I really did not buy a red wig—it is blonde—the same color of my hair that now lies on the floor of Vicki's beauty salon.

21

It had been the proverbial day from hell. There were six weeks of school left, and my second graders had a full-blown case of spring fever—all twenty-four of them. It all started when Keith got furious at Bert for knocking off the wing of the model airplane he had brought for show and tell. Keith tripped him on the way to lunch, and Bert fell on the concrete sidewalk and cut his head. Of course, the infamous Louis tried to get into the fracas, but I glared at him and said, "Remember Mrs. Harvard." Like "Remember the Alamo," "Remember Mrs. Harvard" had become my mantra for the rest of the year to keep Louis in line. Bert's mother had to come up to the school to get him to see if he needed stitches, and she was none too happy with me. At lunch, Alice spilt an entire carton of chocolate milk on her new lavender dress. Most children would take spilt milk in stride, but Alice is as prissy as a peacock and a drama queen to boot. She had a pure-in-tee fit until I called her mother to bring her some fresh clothes. Her mother was not happy and neither was I. Then to top it all off, during my sole break for the day, Betty Louise's mother showed up in a snit because her precious daughter did not get a solo in the end-of- the-year music program. "It just isn't fair," Betty Louise's mother whined, "because everyone knows Betty Louise has the best voice in the class."

I wanted to scream, "What's not fair is that my husband is ten thousand miles away in a snake-infested swamp getting shot at and dodging bullets at this very moment." But somehow I kept my cool and talked Betty Louise's mother into going to see the music teacher to air her concerns. The only bright note was that it was Friday.

By the time I pulled my Opel into the carport, I was so upset and frustrated I could have gnawed wood. I had always possessed a strange dichotomy. Even though I could be outgoing, I loved being alone. Even as a child, I was never bored. I could honestly say I never remembered being lonesome in my entire life until Kincaid left. It had also begun to dawn on me that the Army had not just taken away my best friend but jerked the rug out from under my newly discovered sex life. It had been three months since Kincaid left, and I was lonesome and frustrated.

I headed straight to the telephone and called Karen. "Can you get a babysitter tonight? Curt and you have got to get me out of this house—now!"

"Jennifer next door loves Colin and the money. We'll pick you up at seven."

We went straight to the Officers' Club. I was so tense I had barely eaten anything. The base was getting spring fever too, and the bar was packed. Curt could not get me a margarita fast enough. Everybody on base looked out for each other, and several of Kincaid's buddies asked me to dance. For the first time since Kincaid left, I was actually having fun and feeling more like myself. I knew I was drinking too fast and too much, but I could not seem to pace myself like I normally did. I had never been a big drinker because with my petite size alcohol got to me really fast. Karen and Cut would come check on me between dances.

Suddenly, I realized the room was getting a little fuzzy, and I was feeling unsteady. I could not find Karen or Curt, and the next thing I knew I was slow dancing with a man I did not know that well. I vaguely remembered we had met at some time, and his name was Luther. "Luther," I said, "I really don't feel that well. I need to find Karen and Curt to take me home."

"Elisabeth," Luther said, "it's okay. I know where you live." He took me by the arm and led me to the door. "I'll take you home."

"Luther, I really need to find Curt," I insisted.

"It's okay. I'll take care of you. I'll get you home." I knew this was not a good idea, but I was so out of kilter I let Luther lead me to his car. By this time, I also knew I was very drunk, and I could not seem to take any action. As soon as Luther put me in his car, I passed out. When I opened my eyes, we were in my driveway, and I had no idea how long we had been there. Luther opened my door and guided me toward the house.

Willing myself to try and act sober, I said, "Thanks, Luther, I'm fine. I can get in by myself."

But Luther held my arm tighter and walked me onto the porch. Even as drunk as I was I knew there was no way I was letting Luther into my house. I had felt uncomfortable with Luther from the beginning, but now I felt fear starting to form in the pit of my stomach. I sat down on the top step of the porch to try and think. My mind was floating, and I could not get any logical thoughts to congeal.

Luther sat down next to me as he put his arm around me and said, "Elisabeth, I know you must be lonesome. You're so beautiful and sexy."

Immediately alarms went off in all directions. "Luther," I said as firmly as I could, "it is time for you to go. I am fine. Please leave now."

Before I could react, Luther pushed me back onto the porch and instantly was on top of me. He outweighed me by a hundred pounds and was strong as an ox. With one quick movement, he pinned my right arm down and started pulling at my slacks with his free hand. I could smell the strong stench of alcohol on his breath. "I know you're lonesome, Elisabeth. A girl as sexy as you has to be lonesome," he kept saying.

I felt like I was having an out-of-body experience. Surrealistically, it seemed as though I was watching this happen to another person. Finally, I reacted. I started screaming and trying with all my hundred pounds to move, but Luther had me completely pinned. I could feel the wooden boards pushing into my back, and I was seized with complete panic. Luther was a dead weight, and I was having trouble breathing. I was screaming, praying someone would hear me, and gasping for breath at the same time when I felt my slacks rip. Terror and an overwhelming feeling of helplessness completely overtook me.

Suddenly, like a blast of air, the weight was gone, and I took a deep breath. I heard Curt yelling, "You son-of-a-bitch, I am going to kill you." When I finally managed to look up, Curt was straddling Luther and pummeling him with both of his fists.

Finally Karen shouted, "Curt, stop. That's enough. You're going to kill him." She held one of his arms until he stopped. As strong a man as Luther was, Curt grabbed him by the collar of his shirt, dragged him to his car, and threw him in. "If I ever see you within fifty feet of this house or Elisabeth ever again, I swear to God I'll kill you. Get out of here—now!"

By this time, Karen had me in her arms, and I was crying hysterically. Everything became a blur. I vaguely remembered Curt carrying me to my bed, and Karen gently undressing me before I totally passed back out.

I woke the next morning completely disoriented. Slowly, I rolled over and gradually opened one eye and then the other. The clock said nine thirty. I ached all over, and I was positive the Rolling Stones had set up their band inside my head. Then like a mirage appearing in the desert, images of the previous night slowly began to take shape. As the pieces came together, I became physically and emotionally ill.

Karen was in the kitchen making breakfast. Karen and I, each in our own way, always tried to make the world right—Karen by cooking and me by talking too much. "Karen," I said, "how could I have been so stupid last night? What was I thinking getting myself into a situation like that?"

"What is it with you Southern Belles? For all your feistiness and Scarlett O'Hara persona, the guilt factor you girls carry around defies description. Yes, you had too much to drink. I have known you for two years and that is the drunkest I have ever seen you. And yes, it wasn't your smartest move to leave with a man you didn't know that well. But neither of those acts gave that louse, Luther Donaldson, the right to attempt to have nonconsensual sex with you. In case you haven't looked at a dictionary lately that is the definition of rape. So, Elisabeth, I do not want to hear another apologetic word or sigh coming from your south-of-the-Mason-Dixon-line mouth. I've no doubt you have learned a very valuable lesson. Namely, all men are not chivalrous knights in shining armor like Kincaid, but some are jackasses of the highest order like Luther Donaldson."

"Karen, it's a good thing Curt and you came when you did. I was in a state of utter panic even as drunk as I was, and believe me, Karen, I have never been that drunk."

"Oh, I believe you. You know how crowded the club was, and Curt and I had danced almost every dance. I realized I hadn't seen you in a while and went searching for you. Bob Peterson told me he saw you walk outside with Luther Donaldson, and you didn't look like you felt too well. I immediately became alarmed. Curt and I have never liked or trusted Luther Donaldson. I told Curt, and we rushed out looking for you. Luther lives on base, so we assumed he had taken you to your house. I'm just glad Curt didn't kill Luther. We love Kincaid and you, Elisabeth, as much as family."

"I love you both too. Karen, what if people find out about this?"

"Curt and I have already had that discussion. He is going to threaten Luther within an inch of his life if he is seen within fifty feet of you. Curt will also make him think he will report him, so you can rest assured not one word will come from Luther's sorry mouth. You know Curt and I will take it to our graves, so you don't need to worry. It ends right here."

"You know I will tell Kincaid but, of course, not until he gets home." I talked about Kincaid coming home often. It was a ploy to help me keep my sanity. "I have never kept a secret from him, and I am not going to start now. You know, Karen, if I had not been so drunk, I might have had the presence of mind to rip my wig off. That would have stunned that creep Luther Donaldson!" In spite of the seriousness of it all, we could not help but laugh at that amusing picture.

To distract me, Karen changed the subject. "I still can't believe you have only had sex with Kincaid."

"Well, Karen, it was worth the wait. The man is purely amazing in bed."

With a wicked smile, Karen said, "And that would be compared to what?"

"Karen, if my head did not hurt so badly, I swear, I would throw this coffee cup at you. Besides, you owe me big time. If you will recall, I saved your marriage."

"That you did, Elisabeth," and Karen walked over, put her arms around me, and let me have a much deserved meltdown.

22

It had been a long five weeks, but I was starting to see light at the end of the proverbial tunnel. With the help of Karen and Curt, I had made my peace with the Luther Donaldson incident and sworn I would never get into a situation like that again. I had managed to get into somewhat of a routine and started going out with girlfriends more often. Mary Kate and I had taken a girls' trip to Perdido Key outside Pensacola. Her parents had friends who owned a small house there, and they let us stay in it for the weekend. We drank wine, lazed in the hammocks, took long walks on the beach, and talked. Mary Kate was thinking about letting Bruce move back in as soon as school was out. She thought her summer vacation would give them time to see if they could get their marriage back on track. At this point, I was smart enough to realize Mary Kate did not need any more advice, just someone who would listen—so I kept my mouth shut and listened. Mary Kate could not believe I had actually shaved my head, but loving drama even more than I did, she thought it a magnificent gesture. I confided in her about the gut-wrenching Luther incident, and she could not have been any kinder or more supportive. I was slowly gaining some equilibrium in my life.

In the beginning after Kincaid left, I had tried to keep up with the events in Vietnam, but I could not watch the news on television without getting upset and found myself skimming the newspaper articles as I would get so unsettled. I was aware President Nixon was in the midst of major U.S. troop withdrawals. I also knew extensive bombing had begun a few weeks ago in response to an all-out North Vietnamese offensive.

Anti-war protests in America were at an all-time high. When I did let myself think about it, I realized Kincaid would be involved in military intelligence support for the South Vietnamese Army, but I just could not think about this personal war in any depth for any prolonged period of time.

It was a Thursday afternoon, and I had stopped to pick up a few groceries for the weekend. I was thinking to myself that the year was almost half over, and in seven more months Kincaid would be home. I only had a week of school left, and my parents and I had made plans to go to Panama City Beach for a week during the summer. Then I pulled my Opel into our driveway. Sitting on the front porch were two Army officers. Everything stopped. I could not feel my heart beating. I could not feel myself breathing. My first thought was denial. I thought if I did not get out of this car those officers could not say any words I could not bear to hear. Finally, I got out of the car as the world moved in slow motion. The two officers were standing as I approached the porch. "Mrs. Patterson, I am Major McGuire, and this is the chaplain, Captain Stanford. Your neighbor told us you usually got home around this time, so we decided to wait. May we come inside?"

"Yes, of course, please come in," I said as I unlocked the door. My hands were starting to tremble, and I was having trouble getting my breath. "May I get you something to drink?" I asked as they took a seat on the sofa.

"No, ma'am, we're fine, but thank you," Major McGuire answered. Looking me straight in the eyes and with the kindest manner, he said, "Mrs. Patterson, your husband, First Lieutenant Kincaid Patterson, was on a military reconnaissance mission in the Quang Tri Province. There has been heavy fighting in this area as a result of the latest North Vietnamese offensive. The helicopter he was riding in was shot down. Because Quang Tri

Province is presently in enemy hands and because of the heavy fighting in the area, we have been unable to determine what happened to First Lieutenant Patterson and the five other men with him in the helicopter. Our military intelligence is making every effort to find them. As of now, the Army has listed all six men as missing in action. Of course, our hope is that they survived the crash, were taken as prisoners of war, and we will be able to locate and rescue them. Mrs. Patterson, I must be honest with you. We really do not know anything with certainty, but I will tell you this. The Army is monitoring the situation daily and doing everything in our power to find out what happened to your husband and the other soldiers."

Slowly as Major McGuire was talking, I had steadied myself and the realization hit that Kincaid was not dead but missing in action. The relief was overwhelming. Major McGuire was giving me hope, and I gladly grasped hold of it like a butterfly clinging to its cocoon. "Major McGuire and Captain Stanford, thank you. I know this has to be a very difficult job for you. Kincaid has to be alive. I just know it."

For the first time, Captain Stanford spoke. "Mrs. Patterson, my door is always open to you if you need any assistance or just to talk."

"Thank you, Chaplain. I do have a request. Would you please say a prayer right now for the safety of my husband and the other soldiers?" As Captain Stanford prayed, tears of relief and fear ran down my face. I wiped them away quickly as I wanted so much to appear strong to these kind men. I really could not imagine how hard their job must be.

As they stood to leave, Major McGuire shook my hand and said, "Mrs. Patterson, I want you to know something. Your husband is a highly respected man on base. He is a very fine soldier, and the Army will do everything in our power to find out what has happened to him."

"Thank you for those kind words, Major. My husband is indeed the finest man I know. He just has to come home."

After Major McGuire and Captain Stanford left, I sat on the sofa in limbo. I had no idea how long as time ceased to exist. When I first heard the news, I was so thankful Kincaid might be alive that the reality that he might not be had not materialized. But the thought of Kincaid being in a POW camp made me physically ill. Loud knocking at the door brought me back to reality. It was Karen and Curt, and I fell into their arms weeping, weighted down with all the pain and uncertainty of the future. I had lost count of the number of times my friends had kept me afloat these long months.

I went home to Hillston, and we took a family vacation to Panama City Beach for the first time in several years as we had planned. Stewart was home from the University of Florida for the summer and had finally turned into a quasi-human being. We went to Miracle Strip Amusement Park and rode the roller coaster until I was dizzy and ate caramel-covered candied apples and fluffy, pink cotton candy until I was sick. I read every book I could get my hands on and spent days curled up on Grandmother Reid's flowered, chintz-covered love seat playing my childhood games and relishing in her calming presence. Queenie, as always, cooked all my favorite foods even though, in my misery, I had little appetite, but licking those pound cake beaters gave me such a sense of comfort and belonging. It was exactly what I needed.

23

Since Kincaid had left for Vietnam, I had started calling Samson every few weeks. It gave me comfort to hear his booming voice. After talking to Samson, the world seemed a little more right, and I felt Kincaid was closer. Samson had taken the news about Kincaid missing in action very hard as Kincaid was like a son to him, especially since Thelma and he had been unable to have children of their own. We were both trying to be brave for each other, and I could tell he was very glad I was in Hillston for the summer.

One Tuesday morning in July my mother woke me up at six o'clock to tell me Samson was on the telephone. Alysee had been out of jail not quite a year and already had another undesirable man living with her. Alysee's addiction to alcohol and sorry men was unsurpassed. Late Monday night they were driving home from a bar. Her latest boyfriend was driving, lost control of the car on a wet road, and ran headlong into a tree. They were both killed instantly. "Well, Samson, they won't even have to embalm Alysee. That woman had ice water in her veins." It was not one of my finer moments, and I knew Grandmother Reid would not have been happy with me, but Alysee had hurt Kincaid so badly it was difficult for me to have any charitable thoughts about her. "Should I come to Pascagoula?" I asked.

"No, Elisabeth, it's not necessary. It will be a simple graveside service. The shrimpers and their families will come out of respect for Barrett and Kincaid. I know Kincaid told me he took what few things he wanted from his house when he left for West Point. As you know, he made a clean break." This was the first time since Kincaid had left that I was relieved he was not here. I was thankful he would not have to deal with any of this. Then Samson said, "There's not a day that goes by that I don't miss Barrett. It is like a constant ache inside of me. Even after all these years, some days I still can't believe he's gone. Barrett and I were closer than brothers. Kincaid has to come home, Elisabeth." I heard Samson's strong voice start to break.

"He will, Samson," I answered. "I have to believe that he will." I was using all my strength to keep from bursting into tears.

"Did Kincaid ever tell you much about Barrett or his family?"

"Not really. We had such a whirlwind romance, and then when he did talk about his father, it was so painful I never really pushed him. I knew almost nothing about Alysee until she passed out on our bed two months after we were married." I could sense Samson needed to talk. "Tell me about Kincaid's father, Samson."

"He was something, Elisabeth." I could hear the pride in his voice. "He was so intelligent. Barrett loved books as long as I can remember. His favorites were *The Old Man and the Sea* and the *Odyssey*. Can you imagine a Mississippi shrimper in love with the *Odyssey*? He would quote passages to the men while we were out on the shrimp boat. Another favorite of his was "The Rime of the Ancient Mariner." I can still see Barrett standing on the deck with his dark hair blowing in the salty sea air and his steel blue eyes glistening looking all the world like Ulysses in the *Odyssey* while quoting the ancient mariner in his deep, baritone voice. All the men were mesmerized."

"That is amazing, Samson. It's unfortunate he never got to finish his education."

"It's a strange thing, Elisabeth. All the men in Barrett's immediate family died at age thirty-nine." A jolt went through me. "After high school, Barrett had enrolled in a small college near Pascagoula and was determined to work his way through school. He had three younger siblings—a sister and two brothers. That summer his father died suddenly of a massive heart attack at age thirty-nine. Barrett was eighteen, Betty Jean sixteen, Mac fourteen, and Troy twelve. Barrett's mother was never the same after she lost her husband. She grieved herself to death and died three years later. Barrett had to take over the shrimp boat and pretty much try to raise those young'uns by himself. Betty Jean married at nineteen, not long after her mother's death, and went off to live in Ohio. She died of breast cancer three years after Barrett died. She did have one son, but no one ever saw him after Betty Jean's death. Mac moved to Louisiana and took up shrimping. He married for a short time but divorced with no kids. Four years after Barrett's death, at age thirty-nine, Mac died in an accident at sea. Troy, the youngest, bore the brunt of losing his father. He was at the rebellious adolescent age, and his mother, in her grief, basically overlooked him. He was constantly in trouble and ran away at age sixteen. It took Barrett and me three weeks to track him down. He was living with some rough men on the Louisiana delta and refused to come home. Troy was already in danger of becoming an alcoholic. Word would come about Troy every few years—he was always moving around. About a year before Barrett died, he and I went to Louisiana to try and find Troy. Barrett always felt guilty about Troy—like he had failed him in some way. No matter what I said to Barrett, it was something he never made his peace with. After a week, we finally located Troy in a run-down shack way back in the Louisiana woods. He would wake up just long enough to fill up on liquor again. We left a way to get in touch with us with an old drinking buddy of Troy's. Six years after Barrett died, I got a call that Troy had died of cirrhosis of the liver. He was thirty-nine years old. It's hard to imagine, Elisabeth, that Barrett and Troy came from the same parents. I guess it is the age-old story of Cain and Abel."

"It's a mystery, Samson, but Kincaid is as fine a man as his father was."

I heard Samson sigh. Ready to change the subject, Samson said, "Elisabeth, Alysee had pretty much trashed the inside of the house. If it's okay with you, Thelma and I will go through everything. If there is anything we think ya'll might want, we'll send it. I am pretty sure Alysee never bothered to make a will. With your permission, we'll sell the house and send Kincaid and you the money."

"That would be a huge help not having to deal with the house, but Samson, you have to keep a portion of the money for your time."

"Elisabeth, you know I can't do that."

I hesitated. "What is Thelma's birth month?" I asked.

"She was born in October." I heard the puzzlement in Samson's voice.

"Samson, go to a jewelry store and buy Thelma a pretty opal necklace and ring. Opal is the birthstone for October. Then send her a dozen red roses—no, make that two dozen—for no reason. Use some of the money from the sale of the house. Trust me on this, Samson. Every woman loves jewelry and flowers. I don't care what they say."

"Elisabeth, you do know you're an angel."

"Samson, you have the distinction of being the first person to ever call me an angel!"

24

I returned to Columbus a couple of weeks before school started. My mother was against it, but I was determined to spend my second wedding anniversary in Kincaid's and my home. Besides, I had become attached to our new oven although I had obtained it in an unorthodox manner. Mother wanted me in Hillston for my birthday, and she also thought it would be too hard on me being alone. But once again, Karen and Curt came to the rescue. Karen made plans to take me clothes shopping, and then Curt was going to meet us at our favorite Mexican restaurant. As Karen so succinctly put it, "Elisabeth, if you insist on not eating enough food to keep a bird alive, you need to buy new clothes. The ones you are wearing now are hanging on you like a scarecrow. If it takes all day, we are going to find jeans to fit that skinny butt." I was petite by nature, and whenever I got stressed my appetite went out the window. Because Karen was larger boned and a fabulous cook, she had to constantly watch her weight. I was always telling her I envied her natural beauty, and she was always telling me she envied my skinny butt. We made a great team.

The morning of our second anniversary I was having coffee in the kitchen when the doorbell rang. A little surprised to hear someone at my door this early, I opened it to see Roy, the teenage florist delivery boy of last year, standing on my threshold holding a vase containing two red roses. After the initial shock, I fell completely apart. Roy and his hair had grown a few inches in the past year, and once again, he awkwardly stood there holding my two beautiful roses. I was weeping and blubbering at the same time. Finally managing to calm down, I took those gorgeous roses and clasped them to me. "Roy," I said, "let me give you a word of advice. If you want women groveling at your feet for the rest of your life, become a romantic."

The look on Karen's face was something to behold when she saw those roses. She could not believe Kincaid had thought of something so incredibly beautiful. Karen, Curt, and I always spoke as though Kincaid was a POW. We never let the thought be voiced that he might not be alive. Even though it had been three months since Major McGuire sat in my living room, I refused to entertain any other reality. There were signs all around that this heart-wrenching war was winding down with peace talks in Paris and troop pull-downs, and I was determined to not let my hope waver.

Karen and I enjoyed a silly girls' afternoon of shopping. No one could be more fun to be around than Karen; she was the perfect antidote. We had a delicious meal topped with sangrias, and even Curt was surprised and mightily impressed with Kincaid's roses. After I wrote Kincaid and fell asleep that night, I had the most wonderful dream. I was walking down the aisle of the First Methodist Church of Hillston, clad in my hand-beaded satin wedding gown, on the arm of my distinguished-looking father. Try as hard as I could, I could not see the end of the aisle because all the smiling people in the pews were blocking my view. As we came to the end of the red-carpeted aisle, my father stopped, took my face in his hands, gently kissed me, and walked away. As I slowly turned, there standing by the altar was Kincaid dressed in his Army fatigues with his thick, black hair and dark eyes shining surrounded by thousands of red roses.

25

August 22, 1972
Tuesday night

Dear Kincaid,

Happy Anniversary! When I opened the door this morning and saw Roy (yes, the florist still has the same teenage delivery boy) standing there holding two red roses, I lost it. I mean completely, on all levels, lost it. Poor Roy—it will be a miracle if he ever marries after his two encounters with me.

Kincaid, those two roses are the most romantic things I have ever seen. Karen and I are still in dismay that you came up with such a beautiful gesture. The florist told me you came in before you left for Vietnam and made all the arrangements. But most of all, to me it was a sign from God you are still out there somewhere. I know you do not believe in signs from above, and we are not going to argue about it in this letter, but I know it was God sending me a message. They are absolutely beautiful! The florist assured me she got the freshest roses she could find as she was quite taken with you and your grand gesture.

Karen took me shopping and made me buy some clothes. It seems I have lost weight, and as Karen pointedly said, "You look like a scarecrow." You know Karen and her honesty. That has not changed one bit since you have been gone! By the way, I measured my hair the other day. It is a little over two inches! After our shopping spree, Curt joined us, and we ended the night with dinner at our favorite Mexican restaurant. The sangrias have made me a little melancholy but looking at my two roses has renewed my hope.

I just heard that the last U.S. combat troops are departing Vietnam. I won't go into the irony of that. If you were not in a POW camp, you would be coming home four months early. Stay safe, Kincaid, until you get home to me. Your place is saved.

I love you deeply,
Eliza

P.S. I realize math is not my strong suit, but by my calculations you still owe me 1272 roses. I will cherish the scent of every one of them.

26

It was Friday afternoon toward the end of September, and I was on my way home from work. It had actually been a good week after all the orientation and hubbub involved in the start of a new school year. Though school was going well, I was not. In spite of the good school start, I was experiencing an unusual disquiet. Though I could not fathom the thought of anything happening to Kincaid, the uncertainty was wearing on me. Kincaid had been missing in action for four months now. Uncertainty has an insidious way of eroding your being. I thought I had acquired a degree of equilibrium in my life these past months, but I felt that equilibrium starting to tilt, and the layers of fear were piling up inside of me. I had never been prepared for the worst in my entire life, but I let the uneasy thought enter that I might need to start now.

I had dropped my school bag when the telephone rang. I debated for a moment whether to answer it, being so out of sorts, but then I thought it might be my father, as he had started taking Friday afternoons off, and picked the phone up on the fourth ring. As I said, "Hello," I heard an intake of breath, a pause, and then a familiar voice said faintly, "Oh, God!" I froze and for an instant my world stood still. Then the voice I loved more than anything in this world said, "Eliza, it's me, it's Kincaid." I would have doubted my senses, but no one else in the entire world called me Eliza—it was our unique secret. I started hysterically sobbing and screaming all at once.

"Kincaid, I can't believe it. Is it really you? Say something—anything—so I can hear your voice!"

"I love you more than I ever thought possible."

"Where are you?"

"I'm in the Army hospital in Japan. The South Vietnamese Army recaptured Quang Tri last week. We were rescued from a POW camp a few days ago. The good news is I have all my arms and legs. Other than looking like I spent the last four months starving in a POW camp, I am fine."

"I haven't eaten a bite since you left, so we should be just fine." Still crying, I said, "Kincaid, I can't believe it. I could strangle you. You have no idea what you have put me through this past year."

"Elisabeth, sweetheart, this may come as a real shock to your saccharine sense of right and wrong, but the Viet Cong did not exactly put us up in the Ritz." And then finally I laughed, still hysterically, but laughing. Kincaid said, "That is the most beautiful sound I have heard since I walked out of our bedroom nine months ago. I really am sorry, Elisabeth, but I have to get off the phone. The Army still has their protocol, prisoner of war or not. They say I have to stay in the hospital for two more weeks for observation and then I'll be home."

"Kincaid, I thought I loved you before, but you have no idea of the depth of my feelings. I did not even realize it myself."

"Since you like lists so much, why don't you start making one of all the ways you are going to show me this newfound love."

Mischievously I said, "I'll give you one guess what will be at the top of that list, and it won't be baking lasagna."

I do not know how long I stood in my living room cradling the phone, my heart pounding, and tears of joy streaming down my cheeks. I called my parents first. My father answered and hearing his beloved voice I started crying again. Thinking the

111

worst, having feared it all these months, he said, "We'll be right there, Elisabeth, honey."

"Daddy," I whispered, "Kincaid's alive. I just talked to him. He'll be home in two weeks." For only the second time in my life, I heard my father cry—the other being right before he walked me down the aisle of the Hillston First Methodist Church.

"Elisabeth, I want you to know I think Kincaid is one of the finest and most honorable men I have ever met. I thank my lucky stars you two found each other."

"I think the next time you see Kincaid would be a great time to share those sentiments with him."

My father laid down the phone to deliver the momentous news to my mother, and I could hear her joyous laughter in the background. I heard someone pick up the other telephone. "Elisabeth, this is your mother."

"Really, Mother, I thought Daddy had moved in with another woman."

"Ah, Louise, do you hear that?" my father said. "Sarcasm— Louise, we have our Elisabeth back!"

"Elisabeth Belle," my mother said, "go get something to eat right now. I have not wanted to say anything, but you have gotten too thin."

"Mother, I am on my way to Woolworth's to order the biggest hot fudge sundae with double whip cream I can devour. I'll have them put two cherries on top."

"Eat one every day until Kincaid gets home!"

As soon as I hung up the telephone, I jumped in my little gold Opel and sped to Karen and Curt's house taking the curves on two wheels. I really wanted a policeman to stop me as I thought it would be grand to share my incredible news with a stranger, but of course, a policeman never stops you if you actually want them to. I ran into Karen's house screaming the news like a mad woman. Karen and I grabbed each other and danced a combination polka and jig in the middle of the living room. All the sudden commotion scared poor little Colin to death, and he started screaming. Karen picked him up to reassure him the world was not ending, but in actuality was just beginning. "Call Curt to spread the news. After I eat my double hot fudge sundae at Woolworth's, we are going out to celebrate."

As I was licking the last remnants of chocolate syrup from my Woolworth's sundae, my solidly middle-age waitress with ersatz red hair walked over, slapped the check down on the gold-speckled Formica tabletop, and declared, "I have worked at this place ten years, and I have never seen anyone enjoy the hot fudge sundae as much as you just did."

Eyeing the embroidered name adorning her buxom chest, I said, "Minnie, my husband has just risen from the dead, and I am celebrating."

"Well, I'll tell you what, if any of my three ex-husbands rise from their grave, I'm gonna slap them right back down into it," Minnie harrumphed as she plodded off to wait on another unsuspecting customer.

27

The next two weeks crept by at a snail's pace as I neurotically counted the seconds until Kincaid returned home. I lost count of the number of prayers I offered to God in pure and unabandoned thanksgiving. The day Kincaid came home to me dawned a gorgeous fall day, early for the South. Per my mother's explicit instructions, I had indeed eaten a hot fudge sundae everyday, and Minnie and I had become fast friends as I gained five pounds. My hair was now three inches long, and Vicki had cut it in the new "shag" style that was all the rage. It was short, but it really didn't look that bad, and I had splurged on a new outfit I knew Kincaid would love. Driving to the airfield, my heart was pounding so hard I could barely take a breath. Seeing Kincaid get off that airplane with his mass of dark hair and that aquiline-structured face I loved so much was a sight that will stay forever within me if I lived to be a hundred. I willed the tears back so his first sight of me would not be a tear-streaked mess. He was extremely thin, almost gaunt, but he was my Kincaid, all in one piece. He was greeted by the Commanding General first and then each man in his unit. Finally, he started walking toward me, and we were both running by the time I fell into his arms and let the pent-up tears fall freely. No one could describe that first kiss from someone you love so dearly who deep down you had feared you might never kiss again. Karen and Curt were there with three-year-old Colin, who was gleefully jumping around like a little chimpanzee and calling out "K" with every jump. Even big ole bear-of-a-man Curt had tears in his eyes.

When we got in the car, Kincaid said, "Elisabeth Belle, you are the most beautiful thing I have ever seen, and I love your hair." While I was driving home, Kincaid, in his quiet way, took in his surroundings like a man who had been marooned on an island, which in a way he had. Our little rental house had one scrub oak on the side of the yard, and the other Army wives had helped me adorn it with hundreds of yellow ribbons and a large welcome sign strung across the white wooden porch. "Now that is what I call an official welcome," Kincaid said with a broad grin.

Inside, I had placed bedroom slippers and the newspaper by his lounge chair. "As you can see, your slippers are in place, Professor Higgins," I said, smiling. He gently took my hand as we walked slowly through each room. "I've baked lasagna from scratch, and you will be glad to know I did not even burn the house down this time," I said as we walked into the tiny kitchen. The thought dawned on me if I should ever live in a mansion I would never love it as much as I loved this little rented house. When we reached our bedroom, I softly said, "Kincaid, I cannot imagine how tired you must be. We can wait..." I never finished the words; Kincaid pulled my starved body into his and hungrily kissed me. Nine months without someone whose body you desire with all your being is a lifetime, and we had a lot of lost time to make up. Later, while we ate cold lasagna, I thanked God, yet again, for bringing Kincaid back. I knew there were many who never made it home. There was so much to say, but right now all we wanted to do was relish each other's presence. All that mattered right then was that Kincaid had come home to me.

Kincaid accepted the news of his mother's death with the stoicism I knew he would. He had buried Alysee long ago. He began calling Samson on a regular basis as his brush with death and time in isolation had made him appreciate Samson's role in his life more than ever. The intensity of his anger when I told him about the Luther Donaldson incident was palpable. Kincaid was the type of man that processed his emotions internally, but his jaw was clenched as tight as I had ever seen it, and there was a smoldering rage in his dark eyes. He held me tightly and said, "Elisabeth, honey, you did nothing wrong. You must promise me you will not feel guilty. The entire blame is on that son-of-a-bitch Donaldson. He's not worth killing."

Kincaid never said anything else about it, but Karen and Curt told me later Luther had a black eye and was slinking around with his tail between his legs. Like Curt said, "For all the calm and gentility you witness in Kincaid, don't ever forget he is a shrimper's son."

"Well, I personally think everyone needs a shining knight to defend their honor," I said.

I tried again, in a more passive way this time, to get Kincaid to attend church with me. "If you saw what I saw in the war, you would find it very difficult to believe in anything," he said.

I kissed Kincaid on top of the head and said, "God brought you home—that's enough for me."

Karen, Curt, and I, each in our own way, did all we could to bring Kincaid back to this life. In my way of thinking, a person could not bottle up the atrocities that Kincaid must have seen and ever again experience any semblance of normalcy, so I unequivocally insisted Kincaid tell me about his experiences. I plied him with bourbon and passion and whatever helped to open up his internal wounds. Of course, at first he resisted, but my persistence and love were without equal, and gradually he confided in me. Atrocities like Kincaid witnessed should never be written down, but suffice it to say military men are an exceptional lot. Kincaid and his men were tested beyond what any human should ever be tested, and they came out survivors.

God does indeed work in mysterious ways. Kincaid had never been pampered a day in his life, and the losses he had suffered in his younger life prepared him for war. He built up a wall, as he had in the past, so the inhumanity he experienced would not become a permanent part of him, and he survived. I had been on my own for almost a year, so I continued to run things and make as many decisions as possible to help Kincaid slowly acclimate back into his old life. Though what Kincaid had witnessed would always, in some way, be a part of him, by the next summer our lives were pretty much back to normal.

That same spring the last known POW was released from Vietnam, and there was great celebrating on base. The fact that no American soldier would any longer have to endure what he had endured brought Kincaid great comfort. Military families were always aware of the impermanence of their lives, and that spring Karen and Curt had been transferred to Fort Bragg in Fayetteville, North Carolina. There had been many tears and a lot of champagne, and telling little Colin good-bye had been even harder than I thought it would be. After they had moved, Karen and I talked several times a week, and we had already made a weekend trip to visit. We all knew that it would take more than distance to break our ironclad bond of friendship.

28

After our third anniversary with my three red roses, I decided it was time to start our family. Kincaid and I had talked often of having children, and I knew he wanted them as much as I did, so I threw away my birth control pills and twenty-four hours later I was pregnant. I had to be; my body was going crazy. Loving drama as I did, I was determined to surprise Kincaid with the news. It was not easy, but I hid my tender breasts and morning nausea until my obstetrician confirmed the pregnancy. Using my vivid imagination, I typed out the message "In nine months, you will be a father" and glued it under Kincaid's horoscope in the day's newspaper. When Kincaid got home that night, I was stirring spaghetti sauce. One of the first things he always did when he arrived home was read the newspaper—a habit he had acquired while at West Point. Kincaid had superhuman powers of concentration, and while reading the paper, he did not notice I was peeking around the kitchen corner every thirty seconds. Finally, as he folded the newspaper and started to lay it down, I said, "Did you happen to read your horoscope today?"

"No, I never read my horoscope."

"Well, I read it, and I think you should. You're going to like this one."

"Only if it has something to do with sex," he said as he leered at me and picked up the paper to find the horoscope. It was all I could do to keep from laughing.

"You're a Pisces," I said.

"Actually, I do happen to know that fact," he said.

Kincaid found the horoscope and read a minute. He looked up in total shock.

"My breasts are so tender I can hardly stand for them to be touched, and now that you know, may I go throw up?"

Kincaid bellowed out a whoop and rushed over and swung me around in his arms. I had seen Kincaid extremely happy, even joyful, but I had never seen him giddy. That was the only way to describe it. The man was positively giddy.

"I cannot believe you of all people kept this a secret. When are we due?"

"My love of drama won over my big mouth, and what's this 'we' business? I don't see you throwing up. Our baby is due May 25."

"Does anyone else know?"

"Of course not. You had to be the first to know."

"Who should we tell first?"

We immediately called Karen and Curt and Samson. That weekend we made a surprise visit home to Hillston. Before my father saw us, I had Queenie take in red roses to him with a card that read "Roses are red, Violets are blue. Your baby will soon have a baby too." Now the two most important men in my life were positively giddy.

"Lawd," Queenie said, "I hope this baby has Mr. Kincaid's soft way."

"Queenie," I said "you've hurt my feelings. I thought I was your favorite child."

"All I'm saying, if this young'un is feisty like you, ya'll are sure enough gonna butt heads."

In late October, we found out Kincaid was being transferred to Fort Campbell, which was located on the Tennessee and Kentucky border. Kincaid had already prepared me with the news that a move was imminent, but he just was not sure which base. "Well, at least our child will be born in the South," I said when he told me the news. "We wouldn't want him to be born in a foreign country like the North."

"So you are sure it's a boy," Kincaid said.

"Pretty sure. According to Queenie, if it's a girl like me we will end up in a fist fight every other day, so I'm going for a boy."

I hated leaving my second graders so early in the year, but Fort Campbell was lovely with more flora and lusher scenery. We found a charming red brick, three-bedroom house to buy, and the military wives immediately took me under their wing, especially since I was pregnant. I was lucky to find a job teaching first graders even though I would probably miss the last few weeks of school. Except for the breast tenderness and nausea of the first three months, I had a picture-perfect pregnancy. I only gained twenty pounds, and according to everyone, looked radiant.

Around dinnertime the night of May 24, I started getting the heaviest feeling. I definitely knew this baby had dropped in the last week. I did not eat any dinner and sleep was impossible. Sure enough, around midnight the pains started. My suitcase had been packed for weeks, and I woke Kincaid and told him it was time to take me to the hospital. I wanted to be sure and get some drugs before any real pain started as I had no intention of being brave about any of this. After getting admitted into the hospital, the nurse asked me when my baby was due. When I said May 25, she said, "Well, honey, just because your due date is today that doesn't mean you have to come to the hospital." Please, I prayed, let me be in labor so this lady will not think I am crazy. Just to show that impertinent nurse, six hours later I gave birth to a beautiful, perfectly healthy 6-pound, 10-ounce baby boy.

When I woke up later in the day, the first thing I saw was Kincaid's beautiful head of gorgeous, dark hair. He was asleep. "Hey there," I said and gently prodded him.

Slightly startled, he raised his head. "Hey there, yourself. How's the new mother doing?"

"Is my hair in place, lipstick on? How does my stomach look?"

Kincaid reached over and gave me a big hug and the most tender kiss. "You were right. It's a boy. Why are you always right about these things?"

"Because if I wasn't right, you would be. Then you would get a big head. I like you humble and gentle with just the right touch of arrogance you have now. Bozo has a head full of dark hair, doesn't he?"

"Yes, you were right about that too. How did you know our baby would be a dark-haired boy?"

"I just figured we needed more of your DNA on this earth. Mine is too unpredictable. I haven't decided whether his eyes are blue or dark brown," I said.

"This may come as a surprise to you, but when he opens them we will know."

"I keep forgetting he is not a little pea that grew into a great big beach ball inside of my stomach."

"You'll be glad to know you were one of the lucky ones and delivered a real baby and not a beach ball."

"That's easy for you to say. Those drugs are starting to wear off, and my bottom really hurts. If I had delivered a beach ball, the doctor could have deflated it, and I wouldn't be in such agony. How big is Bozo's head anyway?"

"They say average size."

"Well, you could have fooled me. I think they are lying."

121

"You know you scared me to death. You were screaming at the top of your lungs."

"No way! I don't remember that at all. The only thing I remember is the nurse saying over and over to *push*, and I am thinking *I am pushing as hard as I can*. Man, those drugs are really good. Maybe you could go steal a stash to get us through the first year."

When Kincaid walked into my room the next morning, I immediately informed him, "We have a problem. Our baby is barely twenty-four hours old, and I think Nurse Thistlebottom has already reported me to the Child Protective Services."

"I am afraid to ask," Kincaid said.

"Kincaid, she wanted me to keep our baby in my room all night. I asked her if she knew babies woke up in the middle of the night and cried. Honestly, Kincaid, the meds had completely worn off, and my rear end felt like a herd of elephants had trampled on it. In fact, it still feels that way. My breasts are so swollen and tender I could scream because my milk has started coming in. I had been awake for most of twenty-four hours, and she wanted a crying baby to stay in my room."

"You do realize this isn't just any crying baby?"

"Don't change the subject. I offered to pay her if she would keep him in the nursery all night. She looked at me like I was a monster and stomped out. Do you know there are women out there who do this without drugs? That is just pure insane."

Kincaid came over and gingerly wrapped his arms around me and let me sob. "It's okay, Elisabeth," he said, "I know a good lawyer. I have no intention of raising our baby alone."

The morning I was due to go home, Kincaid strolled into my room. "Good morning, Eliza," he said. "Did you ask the doctor when we could have sex?"

"Well, I'm glad to see you too, and actually, I did. Six weeks."

"You're kidding me, aren't you?"

"This time I'm really not. That is what he said—six weeks."

"Is that negotiable?"

"In case you're interested, I still feel like someone ran over my bottom with a freight train. Have you ever seen a prettier baby than Bozo?"

"You're right again. I never have. I have to assume you are not going to name our son Bozo. I know you're disappointed that his nose is not round and crimson red."

"Actually, I have picked out a name."

"May I be the first to know?" Kincaid asked.

"Garland."

"Garland?" Kincaid looked at me quizzically. "It sounds like a United States Senator," he said.

"Perfect! Since Garland is going to be President of the United States, a senator will be a grand first step."

"Where did you get the name Garland?"

"It is a family name on Grandmother Reid's side. You know how much I adore my Grandmother Reid, and I have a thing for family names. I have always loved being named after both my grandmothers. I think you should start life off with a sense of belonging rather than some name pulled out of thin air. Besides, you're one to talk. There's not a more aristocratic name than Kincaid."

"I am afraid to ask, but what is the middle name?"

"I will make a deal with you. We name him Garland, you pick the middle name, and we will negotiate the sex thing."

"Okay, it's a deal. Being from Mississippi, I pick Bubba. That is a family name of every family in Mississippi, and I say we have sex now."

We didn't have sex then, but we sure didn't wait six weeks. We completely agreed that was the craziest rule a doctor had ever concocted. We swaddled Garland Barrett Patterson in a fuzzy blue blanket and took him home to what seemed like a whole new life. Neither of us had really been around an infant. The first time I tried to change my brother Stewart's diapers, he thoroughly doused me, so henceforth I left him to my mother and Queenie. It was unbelievable that a 6-pound, 10-ounce person could demand so much of your time and energy, but Garland was an easy baby, and I finally threw away Dr. Spock's *Common Sense Book of Baby and Child Care*. As Kincaid pointed out, "When has common sense ever come into play for you?" I just went with my instincts, and Garland and I got along splendidly.

I had turned in my erasers and chalk for bottles and diapers. Kincaid and I had decided we could manage to live on his salary. We thought my staying home with Garland was more important than the money. Plus, we had a double reason to celebrate as Kincaid had been promoted to Captain. Garland, by all accounts, was a very good baby. From the beginning, he had Kincaid's temperament. He was extremely calm, and though Garland laughed a great deal, he could get this very serious look in his eyes as though he was contemplating this world and its inhabitants that he had been suddenly thrown into. I was thrilled he had Kincaid's wonderful demeanor because, as it turned out, he lost all his dark baby hair and turned into a blonde, blue-eyed male version of me. "Well, our next child will have your head of hair," I told Kincaid. "I am determined that magnificent mane will be passed on for generations."

124

29

The next year passed at lightning speed as Garland became a lanky, active toddler. He had a wellspring of happiness always bubbling up inside of him but also showed amazing focus and perception for a sixteen-month-old. He could sit still and listen to me read *The Tales of Uncle Wiggily* or *The Jungle Book* for the longest periods of time. He was so much like Kincaid it was uncanny. In October of 1975, Kincaid received orders to be transferred to Fort Hood in Killeen, Texas. To be honest, I was less than thrilled about moving even further away from my parents, but I was so fulfilled with my life with Kincaid and Garland that I would have gladly moved to the South Pole. Besides, I was finally growing up and accepting sacrifice as a part of life. So I just said to Kincaid, "Well, Texas is still technically the South, even if it is its own special brand of the South." I would come to realize it was a minor blessing that God had landed us in Killeen, Texas.

After a year at Fort Hood, Kincaid's orders came through for his hardship tour. We knew it was coming as it was just a matter of time. He would be leaving at the beginning of 1977 for a year's hardship duty in Korea. I was thankful Kincaid had at least been home for Garland's first two years as it was amazing the changes that had taken place in Garland in those two years. When Kincaid left, the adjustment was easier this time. First, I had Garland, and most importantly, Kincaid was not going off to a war. At the end of that spring, Garland and I went to Hillston for Garland's third birthday and stayed for the remainder of the summer. My parents and Queenie spoiled us both rotten. Garland loved pound cake batter and Queenie as much as I did. Grandmother Reid taught him how to play Old Maid and Go Fish. Garland had, blessedly, always been a sound night sleeper but had given up naps early. That summer he started taking naps again, and my mother remarked, "Garland must be going through a growth spurt. He has been sleeping a lot. I bet he will grow up to be a fine, tall man."

30

Dear Kincaid,

How are you? Because in the eight months since you have been gone, I needed you more than ever today. As you know, Garland and I got settled back in Killeen after our wonderful summer in Hillston. Next week, he starts going two mornings a week to the preschool I was telling you about at the Methodist Church. When we got back to Killeen, I was delighted to find we had new neighbors, Maria and Richard Stephens, who also have a three-year-old son, Jacob.

It has been an especially hot, dry Indian summer even for Texas, so Maria and I took Garland and Jacob swimming at the base pool where they had a great time and thoroughly enjoyed each other's company. When we got home, Garland and I got in the shower. While we were animatedly singing "Itsy Bitsy Spider," Garland suddenly slipped and hit his forehead on the tile. I had never seen so much blood and immediately saw he had a deep gash above his eye. All the blood scared him, and he was screaming at the top of his tiny lungs. Somehow I calmly managed to tie a towel around Garland's head, get some semblance of clothes on, and call Maria. She rushed us to the emergency room where the doctor had to sew four stitches in the forehead above Garland's left eye. It turned out the blood was worse than the actual cut.

Garland had calmed down considerably by the time we got to the hospital, but in the process of putting in the stitches, the

127

doctor had to put a mesh cloth over his face with just a hole for the gash. This must have made Garland feel claustrophobic as he started a new round of screaming and attempting to pull the foreign cloth off. The nurse and I had to each take an arm and leg and hold poor Garland down. It was as traumatic for me as it was for him. In all the activity of the summer, I had seen various and sundry bruises on Garland, but holding him down today I noticed several new bruises. When events calmed down, the nurse said to me, in I thought a rather cool voice, "How long has your son had all these bruises?"

"He has had a few off and on all summer," I replied, "but honestly, I just noticed these." She gave me a very cold, strange look and left the room. I was completely unnerved by the time Maria got us home, and I kept thinking about that nurse and the awful look she gave me in the emergency room. Surely, Kincaid, she could not imagine I would harm my precious child in any form or fashion.

Anyway, Garland is fine tonight and back to his stoic little self. As soon as I got him in my arms, he calmed down and went sound asleep. Kincaid, please hurry home so you can set that unpleasant nurse straight. You can tell her I am a completely devoted mother, who loves her husband and child more than anything on this green earth, and to take that accusing look off her haughty face. Any mistakes I have made with Garland have been out of complete inexperience, and most assuredly, not purposefully. I take him back in a week to his own pediatrician, Dr. Adams, to get the stitches out. Thank goodness, as I have no desire to ever see that emergency room nurse again. Can you tell I have an overblown case of righteous indignation? I guess that comes as no surprise to you! I have a feeling by tomorrow Garland will want to show off his new stitches to the entire neighborhood. On second thought, maybe I should plan a "Show and Tell" party and invite Nurse Ratched to prove what a fit mother I am.

Garland and I miss you terribly. You are the constant subject of our conversations. I have enclosed a picture Garland has drawn for you of himself with his new stitches. Your place is saved.

I love you deeply,
Eliza

P.S. If you'll hurry home, I will let you win in Chinese checkers—at least once.

31

The next Thursday I took Garland to Dr. Adams to get his stitches taken out. Having inherited my vivid imagination, Garland decided with his new sutures he looked like Captain Hook in the story of Peter Pan and dressed the part the rest of the week. Garland still had the bruises of the week before and even some new ones, so when Mrs. Edenfield, Dr. Adam's long-time nurse, noticed the bruises she asked me about them. "Honestly, Mrs. Edenfield, I don't know how Garland is getting all these bruises," I said, and I told her about the accusing nurse in the emergency room.

Joyce Edenfield was a large, matronly woman, and she patted me on the shoulder and said, "Elisabeth, don't you worry one whit about that."

Kindly Dr. Adams came in with his soft voice and softer manner, took out the stitches, and looked at Garland's bruises. "I am sure these are normal, Elisabeth," he said, "your son being the average, active three-year-old. Garland is due a checkup, so I am going to go ahead and order a blood work-up." Garland was as brave as could be while Dr. Adams took out the stitches and Mrs. Edenfield drew blood. It was times like this my son reminded me so much of Kincaid. Whenever I had blood taken, I acted like my arm was being amputated.

Monday morning while I was having my coffee, Joyce Edenfield called. "Elisabeth," she said, "can you get someone to watch Garland for a little while this morning? Dr. Adams would like to talk to you—around 11:00 would be good."

My stomach did a rapid somersault, but I said, "No problem, Mrs. Edenfield, my neighbor will watch him." At 11:00 on the dot, I was sitting in Dr. Adam's private office.

From the moment my father read me the fanciful tale of Peter Pan, I was enchanted. I moved to Neverland and seldom ventured out. On occasion, I was forced into reality—in college when Cameron broke up with me and later when Kincaid was missing in action—but I always found myself returning to the safe confines of Peter Pan's abode. There was a door inside of me, and in my mind, it was a magic door that kept all the ills of the world at bay. From time to time, the door would open a bit as an ill would try to escape, but I always managed to ignore it until I finally pushed it back inside and safely closed the door. The door had stayed ajar the longest when Kincaid was in Vietnam, only to be joyously shut again when he returned to me.

Dr. Adams was looking at me very solemnly, and I suddenly realized Mrs. Edenfield had gently laid her wrinkled hand on my shoulder. "Elisabeth," he said pausing for what seemed like a long tense moment, "Garland's blood test results do not look good." I sat very still. I was having trouble breathing and did not dare risk trying to talk. "I'm sorry, Elisabeth, but there is a strong possibility Garland has leukemia." The door inside me swung wide open with a billowing blast of air, never to completely close again. At age thirty, I was finally forced to leave Neverland for good. "We'll need to test his bone marrow to be positive, but if necessary, I will find a state-of-the-art cancer center for Garland. We will get him the very best of care," Dr. Adams was saying. My face felt wet, and suddenly I realized I was sobbing. Kind Mrs. Edenfield wrapped her soft arms around me and gently patted my back. I vaguely remembered Dr. Adams telling me he would call with all the information and asking me if I wanted them to call someone to come pick me up. All I could think of was getting home. I needed to hear my parents' voices. I could not believe, now of all times, Kincaid was on the other side of the world.

32

The Army gave Kincaid a compassionate reassignment, and he immediately came home. We took Garland to MD Anderson Cancer Center, a top ranked cancer hospital located in Houston, Texas. He was diagnosed with acute lymphoblastic leukemia or ALL as it was commonly called. The head doctor at MD Anderson in charge of Garland's care was a Dr. Vandergrift. Dr. Vandergrift was a short man of barely 5 feet 7 inches, slightly rotund with a wispy goatee that matched his head of thick, white hair, and soft, gray eyes that gazed kindly at the world. His affinity for zanily patterned bowties, plus the fact he was one of those rare men that unabashedly hugged strangers, made me love him immediately. I read that ALL had an over forty percent mortality rate, but refused to let those words enter into the depths of my mind. I convinced myself my Garland would be one of the patients that beat this insidious disease even though his test results had shown him to be in the high-risk group. My husband, who was foremost a pragmatist, was more realistic, but because Kincaid loved me and knew how fragile I was at this time, he did not dissuade me of my belief in a miracle, though Kincaid had long given up on miracles.

Our first minor miracle had been that we were stationed at Fort Hood in Killeen, Texas, which was only a three and a half hour drive to MD Anderson. Then another minor miracle occurred. Two of my parents' best friends were Carolyn and Edward Nichols. My father and Edward Nichols had met in law school and had been best of friends since. Carolyn and Edward had two grown sons and lived in Houston, Texas, in a beautiful, older neighborhood near downtown that was only twenty minutes from MD Anderson. With Garland's initial treatment, we needed to be in Houston for two months, and the Nichols graciously asked us to move in with them for this time and on subsequent trips to Houston. They became our second home and made us feel as loved and welcomed as family. The worst part was being away from Kincaid, but he made the drive every weekend to Houston that he could get away from the base and talked to Garland on the phone every evening.

Because Garland was so ill, time was of the essence, and within two weeks we were in Houston beginning his initial treatment of four weeks of intravenous chemotherapy. With the many blood tests and then the chemotherapy, it was painful to watch all those needles stuck into his miniature veins. But with the calm and stoic demeanor he had inherited from his father, Garland was as brave as any three-year-old could possibly be. He also had to take chemotherapy pills, and as best we could, we made a game out of it all. Because ALL had a high risk of spreading to the brain and spinal cord, the second month he had cranial radiation therapy and then chemotherapy was infused into the fluid bathing the spinal cord. The spinal taps were especially painful, and Garland hated taking all those pills. Garland had inherited Kincaid's and my love of the written word, and I lost count of the number of hours I read to him. Because I had a special affinity for fairy tales, I read them all to Garland—*The Wonderful Wizard of Oz, Alice's Adventures in Wonderland, Peter Pan.* I did all I could to take Garland from his pain-filled world to the land of cowardly lions, talking white rabbits, swashbuckling pirates, and star-lit fairies, if only for a few hours. It was a blessing Garland had inherited my overactive imagination—if ever he needed it, it was now.

When Garland lost all his hair, I told him the story of Jenny. Jenny and I had kept in touch with each other since I had left Columbus. She had just turned thirteen and was a healthy, beautiful teenager. Garland was fascinated by Jenny's story and loved the fact I had shaved my head. I framed the picture of me with my bald head and put it next to one of Garland with his bald head on the table next to his bed. Little did I know that my grand gesture of five years ago would one day become so personal. I kept thinking Jenny beat the odds and Garland would too. It was the only time I had been glad Garland had not inherited his father's mane of black hair because it would have killed me to see him lose that.

We started the hat game. Every few weeks I had a family member or friend send Garland a hat. The expression on his face when he opened a new hat was life-affirming—one of pure joy. He assembled quite a collection—everything from an array of baseball caps, a fireman hat, a police hat, an Army hat to a silly hat with a bright, yellow duck on top and an ebony pirate hat with a lofty, red feather. But his favorite of all was the jester hat Grandmother Reid made for him. The three multicolored points were adorned with large, jingling bells, and he loved prancing around with that brightly colored hat perched atop his bald head, shaking it back and forth. The doctors and nurses that filled his young life were all saints, and they rapidly fell in love with our animated Garland. Even though Garland had no hair, I still thought of him as my blonde-headed little boy.

The rest of the year went by in a haze. Garland was given a few months respite from the intravenous chemotherapy and tested again in March. Even though the results were better, the leukemia was still present and his blood counts were not where they should be. Garland began another round of treatments. The year 1978 passed like an endless roller coaster ride where there were moments of hope followed by days of despair.

Dr. Vandergrift and Garland had established a wonderful rapport, especially for a child so young. I think Garland envisioned Dr. Vandergrift as a kind of Santa Claus. Dr. Vandergrift explained to Garland, "For some reason even doctors don't understand, some bad guys have gotten into your bloodstream, so the nurses and doctors here at the hospital are putting good guys in to help get rid of the bad guys."

"Who's winning?" Garland asked.

"Right now the good guys are doing a pretty good job," Dr. Vandergrift answered as he gently stroked Garland's bald head. One of the beauties of fairy tales is that the good guys come out on top—the frog turns into Prince Charming, the princess gets the handsome prince, the wicked witch evaporates into a hazy puff of green smoke. Being the supreme believer in fairy tales, I kept telling myself the good guys had to win.

33

We tried our best to keep life as normal as possible for Garland. I did not let him win in Candy Land every time, and even at four years old, he knew when he had truly trumped me. One day when we were snuggled in his squishy beanbag watching his favorite television show *Sesame Street*, out of the clear blue Garland asked, "Am I going to die?" My stomach constricted like someone had knocked the air out of me. Garland was so much like his father—astute and wise beyond his years.

I turned to him and said, "Garland, you know you have a very serious illness. The doctors are doing everything they can to stop it. They don't have the perfect medicine yet."

"But can they make it go away, so I can get old like Daddy and you?"

Summoning all my strength, I jokingly said, "Garland, my little lad! Wash your mouth out with soap. You just called your Daddy and me old."

He giggled and gave me a hug. "Well okay, you're not old like Granddaddy and Grandma. You're just sort of old."

"How about sort of young," I teased.

He giggled again and nestled back in my lap. Ever the diplomat, in a few minutes he said, "I don't think you are old, Mommy."

I took a deep breath and said, "They don't have any medicine yet that will cure you forever—just for a time." Suddenly without warning, salty tears started running down my cheeks.

"It's okay, Mommy, don't cry," Garland quickly said. "I have a feeling God and I are going to be best friends."

In our quest for normalcy for Garland, when he was well enough, we took him to Panama City Beach and stayed at the same Grantham Cottages of my youth. They had installed new air conditioning units that now purred smoothly, sending out continuous streams of cold air. I missed the old units that sputtered and spat out irregular gusts of air, but the same black and white linoleum covered the floors—more scratched from years of tourists' sandy feet, but still comforting.

I introduced Garland to the frozen orange taste of Dreamsicles, and he ate his first fried oyster. Kincaid and I laughed with abandonment at the wry face he made as Kincaid snapped a picture. We sat in woven aluminum beach chairs down at the water's edge and let the salty waves wash over our bare, tanned feet. Garland was fascinated at the juxtaposition of the sandpiper, whose gray and white feathers looked like a Jackson Pollock abstract and who moved like an energized robot, to the snowy, white egret, who walked with the stilted grace of a mime. "That sandpiper looks like Grandma trying to keep up with me," he said. Just as my father had done with me, at night Kincaid rocked Garland to sleep with the roar of the ocean in his ears.

We made a trip to Orlando, so Garland could soak in some of the magic of Disney World. "It's a Small World" was Garland's favorite as it had always been mine. All the melodious voices of those colorfully diverse children mechanically moving and singing simultaneously was the ultimate magical experience. Kincaid's favorite, of course, was "20,000 Leagues Under the Sea." We wheeled Garland around in a pint-size wheelchair, and he discovered corn dogs and caramel apples. Mickey Mouse became his new best friend. We bought him a Mickey Mouse tee shirt which he refused to take off for the rest of the vacation except when forced to bathe. It was becoming obvious that Garland had inherited my stubborn streak, but that was a good thing. He would need all the tenacity he could muster to fight this dreadful disease.

Ever since Garland had become ill, Kincaid and I had not acknowledged the future, but lived in the present. We found that it was the repetition of life that gave Garland the most joy. He would ask us to read the same bedtime stories, tell the same corny jokes, sing the same out-of-tune songs over and over. I think it gave Garland a sense of structure and belonging.

In February of 1979, eighteen months from the day I had sat in Dr. Adams' office and heard the words that would forever change our lives, Dr. Vandergrift called us into his private office. I could hear Garland's laughter as the nurses played with him on the other side of the door. With tears in his kind gray eyes, Dr. Vandergrift very gently told us that Garland was no longer responding to any of the treatments, and he felt it would be unfair to make him suffer through them any longer. He told us to enjoy what time we had left with Garland. Truthfully, this was no surprise. Though we had not verbally spoken it, deep down Kincaid and I could both see Garland was not getting any better, but it was earth-shattering to hear Dr. Vandergrift put it into words. Our last ray of hope was destroyed.

"Dr. Vandergrift," I said struggling to contain my composure, "I cannot stand the thought of Garland's last days being in a strange hospital room. May we keep him at home with us until...until the end?"

"Elisabeth, that's not done too often. Are you sure you can handle that?"

Kincaid took my hand and said, "Yes, between the two of us, we can do it. Dr. Vandergrift, we really want Garland at home."

"Yes, of course, you have my permission," Dr. Vandergrift said, and his voice broke for just an instant. I knew he had become very attached to little Garland. "I agree it would be best for Garland to be at his home."

That night after Garland fell asleep, Kincaid said, "Elisabeth, I know you don't want to do this—I know you don't want to leave Garland for even a short while—but I am going to take a few more days off. Your parents would love to watch Garland—in fact it would be good for them. I want us to go to the beach for just a couple of nights, and I want you to cry until there are no more tears."

"Is that even possible, Kincaid—no more tears?"

"Of course not, but we need a few days together. Please, Elisabeth."

I paused. I knew Kincaid was right. "Yes, Kincaid, you're right. Two nights."

We took Garland to my parents in Hillston, and Kincaid and I drove to Destin where we had spent our honeymoon. We stayed two nights at the Frangista Beach Inn. Besides the bedroom, the inn had a small sitting area with a kitchenette, so we would not have to leave if we did not want. I cried until I thought there were no more tears and then I cried more until my eyes literally ached. "Kincaid," I said, "I was so naïve about life. I really believed if I worked hard enough and obeyed all the rules life would do my bidding. Could I have been any more wrong?"

"Elisabeth," Kincaid said, "there is something I want to talk to you about. It is very important to me. I know you believe in God and in an afterlife, but Elisabeth, I don't believe that. I just can't, but I want Garland to believe. I can't lead him there, but I want you to. I want you to give our son faith."

"Of course I will, Kincaid," I said. "I don't know how, but I have enough faith for all of us. It is your strength that I will need."

I had lived in the moment with Garland ever since I had found out about his illness, but now I knew I was going to have to start letting go. But that night as Kincaid and I made love, I held his dark eyes with mine willing our love to make the present last.

34

I n the dark days that followed, all the family and friends woven into the fabric of our life sustained us. Karen, Curt, Mary Kate, Samson—they all came to visit as often as possible. Mary Kate had found a new prince of a husband, Kevin—someone who loved her as she deserved to be loved. I never would have made it without our friends and, of course, my parents. They were just plain heroic. I knew my parents loved Kincaid deeply—like a son—but having us so far away was difficult, especially now. But like my very wise mother said, "As a parent, you do what is best for your children, not what is best for yourself."

Meanwhile, Stewart had grown into a handsome and kind young man—a full-fledged human being. He had chosen the University of Florida for college—presumably to party—but had actually ended up getting a degree and, subsequently, graduating from the University of Florida Law School. Stewart had gone into practice with my father, which made Lawson deliriously happy. He was engaged to be married to Anna Louise, a charming girl from Jacksonville, Florida. "Miracles do happen!" I had told my mother. Being a grown child himself for so many years, Stewart had become quite attached to Garland. The few times I stepped away from my pain, I could see the pain of others.

Queenie said she would have mailed us some pound cake batter if she could have figured out a way, and Grandmother Reid never let me forget that there was a God to give me strength. "Grandmother Reid," I said on one of my more uncharitable days, "if one more well-meaning soul tells me God does not give you more than you can handle, I swear, I am going to put my puny hands around their neck and try to strangle them."

"Child, that saying is just plain hogwash," Grandmother Reid said. "It is the biggest falsehood perpetrated on religion since the days of the Garden of Eden. It happens all the time. But what God has promised is that he will be with us whatever happens to give us inner strength to draw upon. It is up to us whether we let him help us. Some do, some don't. It's a body's choice." That was the beauty of Grandmother Reid. She did not lecture—she just stated the facts according to her wise ways and let you decide for yourself. Then she lived her life according to those tenets she espoused. "But I will tell you this, Elisabeth Belle," Grandmother Reid added, "you have a deep core of strength that you do not even realize, and you have a deep faith."

With the passing days, Garland was getting weaker. We did everything we could to keep him as comfortable as possible. We had ensconced him in our king-size bed surrounded by a colorful array of his favorite stuffed animals, and Kincaid and I took turns sleeping beside him. The previous Halloween, Garland had decided he wanted to be Dracula. I sewed yards of black and red satin fabric into a swirling Dracula cape, and Garland would not be separated from it for the last year of his life. He always said he felt as though he could fly when he wore that cape.

One day as Garland and I were lying in bed together watching *Sesame Street* on television, without warning, I felt tears streaming down my face. "Mommy," Garland asked, "are you crying because I have to leave you?"

Trying to hold my emotion in check, I said, "Yes, sweetheart, that is exactly why I am crying."

"Mommy, you know I won't ever really leave you," my wise son said. Those words would be my saving grace.

It became obvious we were entering Garland's last days. He was extremely weak and sleeping most of the time. The most he could eat was his favorite strawberry Icee from the convenience store, and his breathing had become very shallow. One week after Garland's fifth birthday, Kincaid and I got in the bed and lay on each side of Garland. I put my head carefully on his tiny shoulder and laid my hand on his weakening heart. He was so painfully thin and pale. I must have dozed off because I felt Kincaid gently shaking me. "Elisabeth, sweetheart," he whispered, "wake up. It's over. Garland has gone."

I thought I was prepared for what I knew was inevitable. At least the pain and suffering for Garland would cease. But looking at what was still in my eyes my blonde-headed beauty, so motionless and wan wrapped in his Dracula cape, I realized with heart-wrenching clarity a parent can never be prepared for the death of their child. No matter what I believed about an afterlife, at this moment, the reality was I would never see Garland smile again or feel his small arms hugging me or hear his squeals of joy over some small pleasure. I would never see our son grow into the fine, tall man my mother had predicted he would become. The finality of death overwhelmed every cell in my body and brought me crashing to my knees.

Relying on the inner strength Grandmother Reid assured me I had, I managed to get through the next few days. We took Garland back to Hillston and buried him in our town cemetery surrounded by the love of family and friends. They were all there—the kind people of Hillston who had helped raise me and our new friends who came from different cities and towns. There were no words for a time like this, but words were not needed. All that mattered was that these good people had come to say good-bye to our little golden boy. Surrounded by moss-covered oak trees and the blooming lilac blossoms of crepe myrtles, we laid Garland between his great-grandfather, Judge Sterling, and beloved Aunt Ama, who had raised Grandmother Reid. In the end, Garland was right. He could fly in that Dracula cape.

35

After we buried Garland and got back to Killeen, what I had tenuously held together fell completely and unequivocally apart. A paralyzing ennui descended over me like a shroud, and my heart and soul became encased in a debilitating numbness. There were days when Kincaid kissed me good-bye to go to work, and I never got out of bed. I would lie in a state of inertia clutching Garland's tiny Mickey Mouse tee shirt, crying until the tears would come no more. On the days I did get out of bed, I would wander around in an unfocused daze. Wet clothes would be in the dryer because I never turned the dryer on. Kincaid came home one day to find the orange juice and the cream sitting on the counter from that morning. One night I served spaghetti and forgot to cook the pasta. I was going through the motions of living, but they were only motions. I felt like Alice on her way to Wonderland when she fell down the rabbit-hole. She went down, down, down the dark tunnel and thought the fall would never come to an end. A continuous mantra ran through my head like the clicking wheels of a train on a railroad track. Did I tell Garland everything I wanted to tell him? Did I keep him happy and relieve his fears? Did I do all I could for him? Always Kincaid was there, patiently holding me, letting me sob, helping me put one foot in front of the other.

A watershed moment came that fall. Though I was a less than stellar cook, I had inherited a green thumb from my mother. Garland and I had spent many a happy day with dirt up to our elbows planting bright yellow zinnias, golden marigolds, and purple pansies. As the weather cooled a bit, I returned to our yard and very slowly began to find a healing power in the rich loam between my fingers and the cool breeze and bright sun on my face. Gradually, I found time was helping me forget much of the night Garland died. What I remembered most of that night were Kincaid's strong arms encircling me and thinking I would surely drown in my tears if those arms were not holding me up.

Increasingly with the passing days, I was finding more pain free moments. The hours of needles and chemotherapy—the days of pain and hurt—were being replaced with memories of happier days. One morning looking at the snapshot of Garland that sat on my bedside table eating his first oyster, I found laughter instead of tears. A memory of our family at the beach when we had taken Garland to the pool surfaced. I was sitting on the tile ledge lazily dangling my legs in the tepid chlorine water when I heard squeals of laughter and looked up to see Kincaid in the pool gently throwing Garland in the air and catching him. The water drops were glistening in the sunlight as they scattered in all directions from Garland's sun-kissed skin. One day while planting zinnias in the yard, I had a memory of Kincaid and Garland sneaking up behind me and dousing me with water from the hose. It turned into a full-fledged water fight with Garland and I teaming up and Kincaid screaming for mercy in the end. I was slowly healing. Rather than dwelling on what would have been, I began remembering what we had. Though I had indeed questioned God, even accused him, my faith had not wavered. I began to find thanksgiving in the days we had with our precious son and began to realize that as long as I had these memories, I would have Garland.

As I gradually emerged from my deep, dark tunnel, for the first time in months I really saw Kincaid and what I saw jolted me back to reality. Kincaid had lost weight, and for the first time since Vietnam, there were dark shadows under his eyes. I began to notice that he walked around with an inertia that he had never possessed before. Ever since I had first met Kincaid, he had always lived life with great purpose. One night out of the blue as we were reading in the den, Kincaid said, "Elisabeth, what if there is not a heaven like you believe? What if Garland is nowhere?"

A quiet panic took hold of me. "Kincaid, that is the beauty of it all—that is the essence of faith. You believe in something you cannot see but only sense." I walked over to the chair where he was sitting and put my arms around him and his obvious pain. "Garland is in God's arms now, Kincaid. You need to believe that."

That conversation haunted me, and things with Kincaid did not get better—they got noticeably worse. He became more withdrawn and more taciturn. Finally, I knew I had to take action. One night after dinner, I sat Kincaid down on the sofa and laid down the law. By now, he knew when I was irrevocably serious. "Kincaid," I began, "regardless of what you think, I never want to hear you say there is not a God. God is raising Garland now, and I refuse to think of our child alone. Second, marriages have broken up over the death of a child. I do not think for a second ours will, but I am not taking any chances. I lost Garland to this world—I cannot lose you—it is not an option. Kincaid, you cannot go inside of yourself and grieve alone. I am as devastated as you are. You have to share your grief with me. I need you to do that for me, Kincaid," I paused. "Do I make myself perfectly clear?"

"Yes, ma'am, you do," Kincaid quietly said and then held me in his arms like a drowning man clinging to a lifeboat. I thought I had gotten through to him—I really did.

At first, he tried—he tried so hard. But as the days slipped by, gradually Kincaid began to slip away again. The twin demons of desertion by a mother and father—one by design and the other by fate—reared their ugly heads. The pain of losing Garland brought Kincaid back to the pain of his youth—the wrenching loss of his beloved father and the abandonment by his mother. To his eyes these were all betrayals, and they settled in his soul and took residence with an implacable tenacity. I felt a panic start to take hold of me like the slowly raising waters of a levee during a storm waiting to burst open. All I knew was that I could not lose Kincaid too.

I called Father John at his Parish in North Carolina, where he was now a priest. His wise counsel had never failed me. He told me what I already knew. "Elisabeth," he said, "Garland's death has brought back all the agonies and unfairness of Kincaid's childhood that Kincaid has so carefully tried to accept and put aside. I think he finds some form of strange comfort in having someone to blame. In his mind, there is no one to blame but God even though he doubts his existence. I know this is of no comfort to you, but as we have talked before, Kincaid has to find his own way. Once again, all you can do is wait patiently with your love and be his strength now."

"Father John, what if he doesn't come out of this shell he has built around himself?"

"I believe he will come back, Elisabeth. Your bond is too strong. You are the only life rope Kincaid has." Samson told me the same thing, but their words rang more and more hollow as the days passed, and I watched Kincaid fold deeper and deeper into himself like an accordion that has been latched shut and put on a shelf.

Then my panic began to rise to a new level. Throughout our marriage, our lovemaking had been the one constant. From the beginning, we had been physically and emotionally attuned and had always found solace in each other's arms. With each other, we could find happiness in the midst of deep sorrow, and our bodies and souls gravitated to one another. Temporarily, we entered our own domain and forgot about the unhinged world swirling around outside. There was always passion. It was one way we got our strength—it was what sustained us in the brightest and darkest of days. Kincaid had always been the most attentive and considerate of lovers. Lovemaking was an art to him, and he had mastered it with the skill of a true artisan. It was no accident that I had learned to love sex as one of the greatest pleasures afforded the human race as I had been taught by a master teacher.

The past few months Kincaid's lovemaking had become robotic. He still desired me, of that I had no doubt, but increasingly, I felt like I was making love to a stranger, and panic gripped me like a vise around my heart. I knew things could not continue the way they were and that I had to try and reach Kincaid. One Saturday morning I went into the kitchen where he was having coffee. "Kincaid," I said, "we have to talk. I cannot do this alone. You are being selfish. I loved Garland as much as you did. You are the only person in this entire universe who can share this with me." Kincaid gave absolutely no reaction, and as my panic and fear began to surface, I did what I had rarely done in our marriage and began to scream at Kincaid, "You cannot blame a God that you have never allowed into your life! That is not fair!"

Kincaid did the only thing I never thought he would do. He looked straight through me, got up, and left the room. Through blinding tears, I ran from the house, jumped in my car, and did what I always did when I was hurting before there was Kincaid. I went home.

36

I awoke to the midmorning sun streaming through soft, white eyelet curtains. As I opened my eyes, the first thing I saw was a decade-old photograph of my college roommate Shirley and me at Briarmore dressed as Munchkins in our sorority's musical production of *The Wizard of Oz*. Neither of us could carry a tune in a bucket, so the only choice was to cast us as hyena-laughing Munchkins, which we did splendidly well. All these years, my mother had left my childhood room exactly as it was the day I got married. I found this out of character for my mother as I always thought my father was the sentimental one. But right now, I was thankful to have the comforting familiarity of the past.

I had driven straight through the thirteen hours to Hillston, stopping only for gas, and fallen into my parents' waiting arms. On the long drive I had plenty of time to think, and we sat up half the night as I took full blame. "I realize now how selfish I was right after Garland died. Kincaid was there for me, but I see now I was not there for him. In my pain, I did not reach out to Kincaid like I should have. I had Kincaid, but he had no one." Physically and emotionally exhausted, I had slept off and on most of Sunday. In my ever present optimism, I always believed love and trust would triumph abandonment and loss, but for the first time in our nine years of marriage, I was beginning to fear that might not be true. The terrible realization hit me like a bolt of lightning that Kincaid's natural stoicism had become an armor that kept the pain out but was also keeping me out.

Still weary, I slowly roused from sleep. I could hear the rattling of pots and pans as Queenie hummed one of her lively tunes. The din of low voices was in the background, and I assumed my father had decided to take the morning off. Looking in the bathroom mirror, I saw how thin I had gotten. "I am determined to gorge on Queenie's fried chicken and biscuits," I muttered to myself. "I look like a refugee victim." Slowly, I made my way to the smells of the kitchen where Queenie was cooking, and my parents were having coffee. "Good morning," I said.

They all looked at me expectantly, and Queenie was the first to find her voice. "Miss Elisabeth, I expect you need to get on into the living room."

Puzzled, I made my way into the living room, and my first sight on entering was a beautiful head of silky, ebony hair that looked up at me with eyes so dark they were almost black. "Kincaid," I cried.

With tears in his eyes, Kincaid came to me and said, "Eliza, whatever made you think I could live even one day without you." Pulling me into his arms, Kincaid kissed me with the passionate abandonment of a man who was lost but had found his way. For the second time in my life, Kincaid had come back to me.

37

Dear Kincaid,

This morning in church as I looked at your profile silhouetted by the radiant fall light streaming through the stained glass window, I gave silent thanks to God for guiding us to each other. I need your quiet courage and strength, and I like to think you need my deep faith and my passion for life. I hope I have helped you open your heart to all emotions and fully embrace life.

After Garland's death, there was a place inside of me that was numb and cold. It took time, but gradually with your love and help, I felt a thawing and a tenuous burst of happiness. As painful as it was losing Garland, it was when I thought I was losing you that I felt as though I was suffocating. Now that you are back, I feel as though we have begun life anew, knowing that together we can survive anything.

I have learned to be thankful for every moment we had with our precious golden Garland. Ultimately, it was Garland who brought us even closer, and it was Garland who started you on your journey toward God. In your search, you will not find all the answers as no one ever does, but it is in searching that you will find a deeper faith.

So, Kincaid, take my hand as we continue our journey through this life together. Your place is saved.

I love you deeply,
Eliza

P.S. Kincaid, you might want to read your horoscope today. You are going to like it.

Acknowledgments

For their endless encouragement and support, I give my love and thanks to my family. First, I thank my husband, Tommy, who is the finest man I know and whose place I have saved for forty years. To my son, Tommy Jr., who is my soul, thank you for being my web master as well as a source of great entertainment. To my daughter, Elizabeth, who is my heart, thank you for being my first reader, editor, encourager, and most especially, for marrying Justin, who is a much loved and welcomed addition to our family. Best of all, thank you for the newest member of our family, the love of my life and first grandchild, Oliver, who I am glad to say already loves books.

There are debts of gratitude that can never be repaid and one of mine goes to the incomparable Kathie Clemons Bennett. Kathie believed in me when I did not believe in myself and it is because of this belief and her tenacity that this book is in print. My dear friend and mentor, Michael Morris, has been there from the beginning as he helped me navigate the world of publishing. Gloria Pipkin was one of my first readers and her encouragement has always kept me going. My heartfelt thanks goes to the remarkable Michael Leleux for bringing me kicking and screaming into the brave new world of social media.

Another debt of gratitude goes to the wonderful people at Mercer University Press for taking this book under their wing. Marc Jolley, Marsha Luttrell, and Mary Beth Kosowski are exceptional individuals as well as a pleasure to work with and their support is greatly appreciated.

Thanks go to the many family and friends who had book signings and boarded me in the last four years. I give special gratitude to the world's best book sellers—my amazing sisters,

Beth and Pam, my ninety-year-young friend, Frances Burgess, and the delightful Carol and Eric Nelson, who also produced my incredible son-in-law. To my wonderful town of Panama City, Florida, thank you for embracing one of your own. There is nothing like a Southern town. Trust me on that one!

Much gratitude goes to Dean Resch, who shared valuable information about the Vietnam War and the military. Dean served two tours of duty in Vietnam and, after retirement from the military, returned to Iraq as a civil servant. Dean is battling the effects of Agent Orange and is a true American hero. Many thanks goes to Nancy Neuhaus at MD Anderson Cancer Center in Houston, Texas, for graciously guiding me to Dr. Joann Ater. I am very grateful to Dr. Ater for taking the time out of her busy schedule to answer my many medical questions. My dear friend, travel partner, and "babysitter," Paula Johnson gave me valuable insight into military life as a result of her eighteen moves with four children in tow.

Last, my deepest gratitude goes to Shirley Dunn, a dear friend, for sharing her story with me. Shirley is a woman of great courage and was an inspiration for this book. We cherish the memory of her beautiful daughter Laura.

I love you each.